THE LUCASES OF LUCAS LODGE

CLARA BENSON

MOUNT STREET PRESS

THE LUCASES OF LUCAS LODGE

CHAPTER 1

Miss Maria Lucas, second daughter of Sir William Lucas of Lucas Lodge, had long been accustomed to be considered of little importance among her family. As the only daughter remaining at home—her elder sister having married to distinct advantage two years before, and her younger sister being at present on an extended stay with some cousins—she frequently found that her own claims to attention were overlooked in relation to those of her four younger brothers, who seemed all to have reached the troublesome stage of behaviour at once. To be sure William, the eldest, appeared to hover intermittently on the brink of becoming a useful member of society, but up to now he had shrunk from taking the final step, and he was at present causing his dear mamma palpitations at his insistence on riding the old chestnut mare at a gallop past the drawing-room windows whenever Mr. Thripp, the clergyman, visited. The younger boys were little better, having only the advantage of being too small to run and reach the stable before William, but it could fairly be assumed that once they had achieved the required length of leg and could beat him in the race, they would take the first opportunity to attempt to outdo their brother in mischief.

While Lady Lucas wrung her hands and exclaimed that no woman was ever burdened with such undutiful sons, Sir William, who might reasonably have been expected to watch over his younger daughters with the care that was due to women of marriageable age but regrettably small portion, was instead almost totally preoccupied with the affairs of his eldest daughter. Charlotte had married a man of excellent standing and even better prospects, being as he was the protégé of Lady Catherine de Bourgh, and since their marriage, Sir William, dazzled by the glimpses of grandeur and opulent living that his son-in-law's great acquaintance afforded him, had spent more time than was perhaps strictly necessary in visits to Mr. and Mrs. Collins, during which he was sure of being invited to Rosings Park of an evening and required to make up a table at whist or quadrille.

A young woman of good family who lives in a sociable neighbourhood must necessarily have intimate friends, but here again Maria felt a deficiency. The Bennets, who were the Lucases' nearest neighbours, were still dining out on their great success in having married off three of their five daughters almost all at once. Two of the Bennet girls had made the most fortunate of matches, and all three had removed from Hertfordshire with their new husbands, and had gone far afield, while the two girls who were still unmarried inevitably spent much of their time in visits to their sisters. One of the girls, Catherine, had been Miss Lucas's particular friend, but she was currently staying in Derbyshire with her sister Mrs. Darcy. Thus Maria found herself frequently left to her own thoughts and devices, and while she was fond of her home and her family, and had no particular ambitions to be elsewhere, she did on occasion feel a certain loneliness, and often found herself wishing that *something* would happen, although she hardly knew what. Modest and unpretending as she was, she thought too little of herself or her prospects to hope that she would ever marry—the neighbourhood of Meryton was a small one and the Lucases travelled little—but sometimes, when they attended the assemblies, she would sigh as she glanced about her and saw the same faces each time—Mr. Wilcox with his tremor and his troublesome limp, and the simpering Mr. Jones, with his damp handshake—and wish innocently for some new society to bring something different to look at, and a little interest into her life.

She was feeling particularly discontented one day, having that morning received a letter from her friend Kitty Bennet in which that young lady wrote with great complacency of a ball she had attended at which she had danced with a lord and a knight, and she could not help expressing something of what she felt to the person with whom she happened to be sitting.

'How many young men there are in Derbyshire!' she exclaimed. 'I am happy to hear that Kitty is enjoying herself with the Darcys, but I should be very glad if she would send some of her dancing partners to Hertfordshire, for I am sure she has more than she can possibly need for herself, and we are almost without.'

The person to whom she addressed this remark was Mary King, an acquaintance of long standing with whom she had recently begun to proceed to terms of more intimate friendship. Miss King was a young lady of great importance—in her own view, at least—for she was the possessor of a fortune of ten thousand pounds, which she had inherited from her grandfather, and there were some who said uncharitably that the sudden accession of riches, however modest, had spoilt her and made her discontented, for it was rumoured that during a stay with her uncle in Liverpool last year she had received attentions from more than one respectable man, but had spurned them all haughtily as being not good enough for a woman of such large fortune as herself.

Miss King now sighed at her friend's remark. Truth to tell, she had been thinking much the same thing. As soon as she had inherited her money she had relied totally upon the notion that it would very soon bring her a suitable husband, but two years had passed without her being approached by anyone of great enough standing for her, and she had begun to feel the first naggings of doubt as to whether her fortune were quite large enough. She did not require much: a young man of five thousand a year or so would be the very thing, and of course he must be handsome, and keep a carriage and horses, but as she looked about her it became clear that no such man was to be found in Hertfordshire.

'What you say is very true,' she said in reply to her friend. 'I am sure at the last assembly I did not dance even half the dances, and moreover I might hazard that not one of my partners was below five and forty years of age. What a pity we have never had another militia stationed at Meryton since the last one left. Do you remember it, Maria? How pleasant it was to be able to pick and choose among the young men—and even to refuse the odd one or two who did not happen to suit. Nowadays, if I were to refuse every man who did not please me I dare say I should never dance at all.'

Maria echoed Mary's sigh and put away the letter, for she feared it would only make her discontented and she knew that she had much to be thankful for.

'There,' she said. 'I shall not read it any more, and I shall leave my reply for a day or two, for at present I have nothing to relate—and, furthermore, I fear that if I wrote today I might sound ill-tempered. I do not wish Kitty to think me discontented, when she only means to entertain me with her letters. I shall write again when I have some news to tell her.'

'What, when you have finished repairing the seam of your patterned muslin, perhaps?' said Mary scornfully. 'Or do you mean when the felled tree that blocks the road on the other side of Meryton has been cleared away? Either of those would be excitement enough here at present.'

'I am afraid that is only too true,' said Maria with another sigh. 'Still, who knows what news another day or two may bring?'

'Who knows, indeed?' said Mary. 'Perhaps you will find a rent in another muslin and have to repair that too. A double misfortune will make far better reading than a single, and you will be doing Kitty a good turn by making her feel the benefit of her present situation.'

CHAPTER 2

In spite of Miss King's scepticism, Maria did shortly have news of some interest to send to Derbyshire, for the very day after the above-mentioned conversation, word began to circulate in Meryton that Netherfield Park had at last been let, following the departure of its previous tenants, the Bingleys, more than a year ago. The neighbourhood of Meryton had felt their loss very much, for Mr. Bingley was a young man of amiable disposition, who liked nothing better than to throw a ball whenever the opportunity presented itself, and, moreover, had a good many acquaintances from outside Hertfordshire for the ladies to dance with. With Mr. Bingley departed many a young gentleman and many a fond hope, and Netherfield had lain unoccupied ever since, waiting only for some other rich tenant to add to the entertainment of his neighbours.

As soon as the news reached Lucas Lodge, Lady Lucas set out to find out who the new-comers were, and was almost immediately able to satisfy herself on that subject by consulting her friend Mrs. Philips, who lived in Meryton and could be relied upon to receive the first intelligence of anything that happened to be going on.

Fairhead was the name of the family who were shortly to take up residence at Netherfield, and if Mrs. Philips's information were correct, then they consisted of a gentleman, his wife, and a grown-up son and daughter, neither of whom was known to be married. Maria heard the news with interest, and began to entertain hopes that the new people might be agreeable and that the young lady might be willing to be friends. For Mary King, who was sitting with Maria when Lady Lucas related the news, her thoughts ran less towards the daughter of the house and more towards the son. Should he happen to be handsome and likely to come into a fortune amounting to two or three thousand a year (for she had now all but abandoned the thought of a whole *five*), then here was a chance indeed! She said nothing as Lady Lucas and Maria speculated about their new neighbours at length, but her thoughts ran along pleasing lines and a resolution began to form in her head.

The Fairheads soon arrived, and with them more intelligence. It seemed that until recently the family had been respectable but not rich, and had lived modestly for many years in an unfashionable part of London. Recently, however, Mr. Fairhead had come into a large inheritance for which, it was understood, he had been waiting many years—longer than expected, in fact, for it came from a wealthy but sickly aunt, who had in the end lived to a ripe old age, as is sometimes the way of infirm people, who not infrequently seem to delay their demise deliberately to vex and inconvenience their families. As it happened,

Mr. Fairhead had been fond of his aunt, and had always held that she had the perfect right to live as long as she chose. In return for this concession the old lady had left him her entire fortune, and, following a suitable period of mourning, Mr. Fairhead removed himself and his family to Netherfield Park, with a view to purchasing an estate of his own in due course.

Visits were paid and returned, and it was soon reported that Mr. Fairhead was an exceedingly amiable man and that his wife was most charming. The son was away visiting friends at present, but the daughter was clever and lively, and altogether the family looked set to be a most welcome addition to the neighbourhood—especially since the younger Mr. Fairhead was rumoured to have a private fortune amounting to a total of twelve thousand pounds, while his sister had eight. Maria Lucas thought about them often, but was not to meet them until the assembly next week. Mary King looked forward equally to the event, and they counted the days impatiently and planned their dress with more than the usual care.

It was October, and until then the month had been a fine one, but in the days leading up to the assembly the weather turned, and Meryton was hit by a succession of heavy rains that kept everybody at home who did not absolutely need to go out. At last, on the day before the assembly, the rain stopped and the sun came out, and Maria decided to go into Meryton, for she had one or two purchases to make and, moreover, she wanted to call on Mary King to talk over the important matter of what to wear for the ball. She was later in setting off than she had intended, and so decided to take a short-cut across a field and down a lane which was generally passable only in dry weather. After the rains there was likely to be flooding, but Maria, who was occasionally heedless in such matters, trusted that her stout boots would protect her against all difficulties, and set off with nothing in her head but her errand.

At first all went well: her boots withstood the wet grass and, by skirting a lake which had formed in the middle of the field, she reached the lane beyond without mishap. She had not gone more than thirty yards down the road, however, when she found that the path ahead of her was quite flooded. She had come too far to wish to turn back, and so she looked about her for some means of getting through. Much of the grass verge was still above water, she saw, and she judged that she might jump from tussock to tussock relatively easily and thus pass to the other side. Hitching up her skirts, she jumped to the first grassy mound, and prepared to jump to the second, but alas!—this one immediately began to give way beneath her feet, and she was forced to jump as quickly as she could to the third. The tussock behind her collapsed completely into the water, and she looked to the next one, only to find that she had made a great misjudgement, for the fourth mound was just a little too far for her to reach with one jump, and she was stuck.

'Whatever shall I do now?' she said to herself in dismay, glancing about her. 'I am stranded and it is all my own doing. Oh, why did not I keep to the road, as I knew I ought?'

She eyed the muddy water that surrounded her. From her little island it looked as though the only way out of her predicament was to tuck up her dress and wade through. How Mamma would scold when she returned home! She sighed, and was just trying to decide which might be the shortest route, when she heard a whistle and looked up. Coming along the lane was a young man—a gentleman in appearance—who was walking with his dog, and swiping at the hedgerows with a stout stick. He arrived at the edge of the flooded part of the lane and swirled his stick thoughtfully in the water for a while.

'Come, Striker,' he said to his dog. 'We certainly cannot get past this way today.'

He bent to caress the dog's head, then straightened up and gave a start as he caught sight of Maria. Several expressions crossed his face in succession, of which the most recognizable was a great inclination to laugh. He swiftly suppressed it, however, and looked about him for a way to reach her. In two great leaps he had reached the next tussock to hers—the one that was too far away for her to jump to—and was holding out the clean end of his stick.

'Here,' he said. 'Do you think you might get across with the aid of this?'

Miss Lucas, blushing and feeling very foolish indeed, said that she thought she might. She grasped the stick, and with one jump was across. He held her arm to steady her and then begged her pardon.

'There is not quite room enough to accommodate us both on this patch of grass,' he said, 'but if you would not fall into the water I fear you will have to accept my assistance. Now, you see the next one is much nearer. If you take my hand and we jump together we shall be past this lake in no time.'

As he had said, the next jumps were easy, and very

shortly Maria was safe on dry land, breathless and stammering out her thanks. He waved them away cheerfully, and said:

'I am only happy that I happened to be passing this way, or who knows how long you might have remained there? I hope not until the water had all dried up, however.'

'Oh no!' said Maria. 'I am sure that someone else would have come at last.' But I am very glad that you came at *first*, her eyes seemed to say to him.

'Well, I hope that no harm will come to you after your adventure,' he said, 'but to make perfectly sure, I should advise you to go home directly and sit by a warm fire so as not to catch a cold.'

He then offered to escort her to wherever she wished to go, for even the drier parts of the lane were very muddy, he assured her, but she was still exceedingly embarrassed and so she refused all offers of help and, pausing only to thank him hastily once again, hurried off as fast as she could, full of her adventure and bursting to relate it to Mary King. What excitement! To have found herself in distress and to have been rescued by such a charming and well-mannered young man—handsome, too, if her eyes had not deceived her, although for most of their encounter she had been too embarrassed to look at him directly. Who could he be? And, just as importantly, how long would he stay?

CHAPTER 3

'Why, of course it must have been Mr. Thomas Fairhead you met,' said Mary as soon as she had heard and exclaimed over the story. 'I must say, it was excessively kind of him to come to your aid, for I am afraid to say it, but you look quite shocking, covered in mud as you are. I suppose he must have taken pity on you, but there—I dare say that is just like his kindness, from all that I have heard of him.'

'What do you mean?' said Maria in the greatest surprise. 'From whom have you heard this? Can it be— have you perchance had occasion to meet the family?'

'You have caught me out, Maria,' said Mary, with a smile of satisfaction. 'I had intended to keep my secret until the evening of the assembly, for it would have been such fun to see your face when you saw me and Miss Fairhead walking about together arm in arm, but now I declare you have surprised it out of me. I met Louisa Fairhead on Saturday—quite by chance, for she and her father happened to be sheltering in the library from a sudden cloudburst just as my uncle and aunt and I entered it, and so we were introduced, for of course my uncle has already visited Mr. Fairhead. I believe we took a fancy to one another immediately, and we met again at church on Sunday—by the way, did not you see us together? I was almost sure you must have, and I was rather wishing you had, for I would certainly have introduced you then. We found we had so many things in common that I could hardly bear to be parted from her, and so yesterday I persuaded my aunt to visit Mrs. Fairhead in order to see Miss Fairhead again and further our acquaintance. I had a terrible time of it, for you know how my aunt hates the rain and the mud, and Netherfield is *just* too far away for a walk in inclement weather, but I would not be denied. I always make a point of having my way, you know,' (this said with great complacency) 'and I am happy to say that Miss Fairhead did not disappoint me. We spent the morning together and I am sure are in a fair way to becoming the greatest of friends. I think you will like her, Maria,' she continued. 'She is a very pretty creature—prettier than you and I, certainly,' (here there was a toss of the head and a sort of smirk which said she did not really believe what she said, at least as regarded herself) 'and rather fine, although by no means *too* fine. She has a quick and lively manner, and such a droll way about her when describing her acquaintance—by the way, I wish you had heard her manner of imitating Mrs. Nicholls; I thought I should die laughing!—and altogether I think she is a welcome addition to the neighbourhood. I am quite delighted with her, and am determined to notice her, and you will see that soon it will be as though she had lived here forever.'

Maria, who continually forgot that she herself was the first in consequence in Meryton now that her sister Charlotte was married, and that it was due to *her* to notice Miss Fairhead, while Mary King was nobody, listened to all this with the greatest of interest.

'I am very sorry I did not see you together at church on Sunday,' she said, 'for I should certainly have come to meet her. She sounds very pleasant, from what you say.'

'I wonder she did not tell me that her brother had already arrived,' said Mary. 'She said that he was expected in the country but I did not realize he would be here so soon. He has been staying at Weybridge with a friend of his, a Mr. Sands. Only think, Maria! If he were to come to the assembly tomorrow and bring with him a friend or two. Do you remember what we were saying only the other day? How happy we should be! I have long been resolved never to marry—for what are men in general but fools and deceivers? However, I must confess that it is very pleasant to dance with a charming young man once in a while—even if he does prattle and talk nonsense, for I am not one of those people who look down upon the lighter pursuits, and on the contrary, I think that when enjoyed in moderation they are entirely harmless and can even lift the spirits and do one some good.'

The next few minutes were given over to the important matter of dress, and soon the ladies had settled to their own satisfaction the question of what to wear. In truth, however, neither was giving the subject the full attention it deserved, for each was absorbed in her own thoughts. Maria's mind was still wrapped up in her earlier adventure; she feared that she had forgotten her manners and had not thanked the young man as she ought—but really, she had been so confused and embarrassed that she knew not what to say. How foolish he must have thought her! She hoped he would be at the assembly so that she could thank him again and perhaps make a better impression than the unfortunate one she had undoubtedly made at first.

Mary King's thoughts, meanwhile, ran along entirely different lines. She felt all the triumph of having been first to make the acquaintance of Miss Fairhead, and trusted that she would soon enjoy all the benefits, for that way, she was certain, was the best way to attain her end, which was no less than to marry Mr. Thomas Fairhead, in spite of her avowed intention to remain single—and the fact that she had never met him. True, Miss Lucas had an advantage over her in having already met Mr. Fairhead himself, but Maria was an ingenuous creature and would certainly have no idea of how to make the most of it; no, Mary felt quite safe on that head. *Her* approach was a much more artful one, and consisted of drawing in Thomas Fairhead by first cultivating the acquaintance of his sister. She and Miss Fairhead would become the most intimate of friends, upon which she would certainly be thrown into the company of Thomas Fairhead frequently, and in this way gain the opportunity to attract him if she possibly could—which, she trusted was not beyond the bounds of possibility, for she had been told she was a handsome girl; and after all, what more did a man look for in a woman, than good looks and a captivating manner? Pleasant visions of fine houses and new carriages drifted through Mary's head, and she smiled to herself. Her only doubt was as to whether Maria would win him first, but this she was determined to prevent.

Had Mary but known it, she had nothing to fear in the way of competition on the part of Miss Lucas, for Maria was entirely guileless in such matters and had no idea that any competition was even thought of. Innocent and trusting as she was, she accepted her friend's words as the truth, and looked forward to making the acquaintance of Miss Fairhead in due course.

CHAPTER 4

The evening of the ball arrived at last, and when Maria entered the assembly room with Lady Lucas she looked about her curiously. A single glance told her that the Fairheads were not yet arrived, but she soon discerned Mary King, standing with her aunt and uncle, in conversation with Mr. Wilcox. Maria went to join them, and was immediately engaged for the first two dances by Mr. Wilcox, who then departed to pay his respects to Sir William Lucas.

'I am glad you are to dance with Mr. Wilcox,' said Mary. 'He wanted to dance with me first, but I find him a disagreeable partner, and happily the idea came to me just in time to tell him that my aunt was a little tired, and had particularly requested that I stay with her for the first part of the evening. You will get on with him much better, Maria. You are so much more patient with his ungainly dancing than I should be.'

The music began and the gentleman returned to claim his prize, and Maria did her best to smile through the first two dances, although they brought her little pleasure, for Mr. Wilcox had damp hair and a pink face, and was a determined rather than an able dancer. To her additional annoyance, while the dance was at its height, she heard a little bustle at the other end of the room, and saw that a group of people had arrived, who, to judge from the buzz of excited conversation which immediately arose, could be none other than the Fairheads. She was unable to see much of what was happening, but she glimpsed Mary hastening forth to greet a young lady whom Maria had never seen before, but who must surely be Louisa Fairhead. She wanted to see more, but Mr. Wilcox just then reprimanded her jocularly for her inattention, and so she was forced to smile and attend to what she was doing, for fear of mistaking her steps.

The dance ended and Maria was thankfully released. Her father was talking to one of the new-comers, a pleasant-faced man of fifty, and he called upon her to join them, whereupon she was duly introduced to Mr. Fairhead, the father of Thomas and Louisa Fairhead. Having said what was proper, Mr. Fairhead observed with a smile that he was pleased to discover that there were many young ladies in Meryton, for he had feared his daughter might find living in the country a little dull.

'Oh, no! The countryside is far from dull,' said Sir William. 'To be sure, it is quiet at times, but this is a friendly neighbourhood and there is always something going on. It will be good for all the young people to have somebody new to look at, however,' he went on after a moment. 'The ladies, especially, lament the lack of young gentlemen to dance with, I believe.'

'I fear I am too old for dancing,' said Mr. Fairhead, 'but

I imagine my son will have no objection. He is of an obliging disposition, and I dare say will be only too happy to dance with all the ladies at once if they wish it—especially if they are all as fair as your daughter, Sir William' (with a bow to Maria). 'Have you met my son, Miss Lucas? He is somewhere about.' He turned to look for his son as he spoke.

Maria, blushing at the memory of the day before, was wondering how to reply, when the group was suddenly accosted by Mr. Thripp, the clergyman, who begged Sir William's pardon and asked if he might have Miss Lucas's hand for the next two dances. Sir William readily agreed to the request, and Maria was duly borne off, without anybody's having thought to ask *her* what she thought of it. Thus did she miss an introduction to Thomas Fairhead, who a moment afterwards came over in answer to his father's summons. They were shortly joined by Louisa Fairhead, Mary King, and another young man who was introduced as Mr. Sands, a particular friend of Thomas Fairhead. The two had spent the past few weeks in Weybridge, and Mr. Sands had returned with his friend to stay at Netherfield for some days. Mr. Sands was tall and handsome, and promised well so long as he remained silent; when he opened his mouth, however, the good impression tended to be spoilt by his conversation, which revealed a firm conviction on his part that he knew everything—a defect in his character that was in no way rendered more attractive by the reality of his incorrigible ignorance.

'And here is Miss King,' said Sir William. 'You look quite charming this evening, Miss King. Mr. Thomas Fairhead,' (bowing to that gentleman) 'your father tells me you are fond of dancing. As you can see, you will find no shortage of pretty girls in Meryton. I hope you come prepared to do your duty as a dancing partner.'

'I do indeed,' said Thomas Fairhead with an answering bow, and, taking the hint, turned to Mary and asked her to dance. Miss King hid her triumph and accepted prettily, and the two departed.

CHAPTER 5

After only a few minutes' acquaintance, Miss King was already exceedingly pleased with what she had seen of Thomas Fairhead. Not only was he handsome, but he had an open and obliging manner, as well as an evident affection for his family—especially his sister Louisa, to whom, as far as Mary could observe, he was in the habit of deferring. This was a good sign indeed! Had he appeared to be the sort who *would* have his own way, her intentions with respect to him would not have changed, but she would have approached her task with less enthusiasm, for an unbending husband promised nothing but hard work; a biddable man, however, was what she wanted of all things, and so there was nothing to do but to set about winning his heart—something which, she hoped, could be fairly achieved in an evening or two. She decided to begin with flattery.

'I must tell you, Mr. Fairhead, how delighted I am with your sister,' she said, once they had taken their places in the dance. 'She has quite brightened up our little circle here in Meryton. How pretty she is! Such a clear, delicate complexion. And those eyes of hers! I declare I never saw such a rich shade of blue, or such an expression in them, when she makes one of her droll, clever remarks. How she made me laugh the other day, when we were talking together! I do believe she is the wittiest woman I know.'

'Is she? I am glad you think so,' replied Thomas Fairhead. 'I speak as a brother, of course, but she is certainly clever. I make no pretensions to wit myself—indeed, I confess that sometimes Louisa is a little too quick for me. She quite laughs at me for it. However, I know she means it fondly. And so you have become firm friends, have you? I am glad of it, for I know my father feared she would find Hertfordshire a little flat after London.'

This was a good beginning indeed, and Miss King was about to follow up her advantage when she saw that Mr. Fairhead's attention had been caught by something. It was Maria, who was just then going down the dance with Mr. Thripp.

'Who is that young lady?' said Mr. Fairhead. 'I met her yesterday, I believe, but not under such circumstances as to allow us to be introduced.'

'That?' said Mary King. 'That is Maria Lucas, the daughter of Sir William Lucas, whom you met just now. Ah! Then you must be the gentleman who rescued her from her absurd predicament yesterday.'

Mr. Fairhead admitted that that was the case.

'It was fortunate that you happened to be passing,' went on Mary, 'or who knows how long she would have remained there? Maria is a particular friend of mine, and I never think of her but with affection, for she is good-natured enough, but there is no denying that she is an empty-headed creature. Her mamma quite despairs of her, for she is always getting into some scrape or other.'

'Well, I am glad I was able to assist her,' said Mr. Fairhead. 'It does not do to remain outside in the cold and wet at this time of year. Perhaps she ought to have stayed at home instead of going out in all the mud we have seen lately.'

Seeing that he was still inclined to look towards Maria, Mary cast about for a means of returning his attention to herself, and was struck by a happy idea.

'Do not concern yourself,' she said. 'She is foolish now, but she will do well with a little more education and worldliness—and those she will get once she is married.'

'What? Then she is engaged?' said Mr. Fairhead. 'To whom?'

'You see her dancing with him now,' said Mary. 'Mr. Thripp is the fortunate man who has won the hand of Miss Lucas. At least,' she lowered her voice, 'that is what we expect to hear any day now. You understand, of course, that the matter must remain confidential until it is officially announced.'

'Oh, certainly,' said Mr. Fairhead, looking again towards Maria. She was at that moment blushing and smiling at Mr. Thripp, and it certainly did look as though there were some intimacy between them. After a moment he recollected himself and what was due to his partner, and the dance proceeded pleasantly until its conclusion.

Mary had hoped that Thomas Fairhead might be induced to remain in conversation with her when they left the floor, but she was immediately asked to dance by Mr. Sands, and, not wishing to appear disobliging before his friend, felt she must accept. Fortunately, Mr. Sands was far too fond of the sound of his own voice to require much conversation from her, and so she had plenty of opportunity to reflect on the results of her first attempt to ingratiate herself with Thomas Fairhead. As far as that went, she had no cause to feel any dissatisfaction. He had seemed pleased with his partner—she was *almost* sure she had discerned one or two glances of admiration, for she knew she was looking well—and altogether he had shown no disinclination for her company. The falsehood about Maria and Mr. Thripp had come to her on the spur of the moment, and she half-regretted it, but on further reflection decided that there was no harm in it—after all, she had not said that they were absolutely engaged, only that an announcement was expected. And in any case, it was as well to remove all expectations at once, just to make quite certain that no attraction could develop—for, after all, the circumstances under which Mr. Fairhead had first met Maria *could* be said to be romantic, and there was no saying how susceptible he might be to such nonsense. If he believed that Maria's heart were already given to another, however, then it was more than likely that he would dismiss her quickly from his mind.

As Mary's thoughts ran complacently along these lines, she happened to look round, and was surprised and not a little vexed to see Thomas Fairhead leading Maria Lucas to the dance. Evidently her information had not been enough to discourage him—but of course, she recollected, since Maria was first in consequence in Meryton, it must not be said that she had been overlooked, and no doubt the elder Mr. Fairhead had reminded his son of his duty. It was no matter, however; Maria was far too stupid a creature to see an advantage even when it stood before her—and besides, while she might be the daughter of a knight, her father had no fortune to give her. Mary remembered her ten thousand pounds and felt safe.

CHAPTER 6

But Miss King was wrong in her supposition that Thomas Fairhead had asked Maria to dance only on being reminded of it by his father, for Mr. Fairhead had had every intention of being introduced to Miss Lucas and of dancing with her. The first was effected easily enough, and Miss Lucas seemed to have no objection to the second, and very soon they were standing on the floor together, and Mr. Fairhead had ample opportunity to admire the delicate flush on Maria's cheeks, which was due partly to her having danced several dances in a row, and partly to embarrassment at the memory of her adventure of the day before.

'I hope you did not take a chill yesterday,' said Mr. Fairhead. 'And I trust you had not been there too long when I arrived. I wish I might have come earlier, that you might have been helped sooner.'

'Oh! I am quite well, thank you,' said Maria. 'And I had not been there above five minutes when you came. It was foolish of me, I know, to try and cross that way, but I fear

I am too impatient sometimes. Mamma often scolds me for my heedlessness. How funny you must have thought me!'

Mr. Fairhead was about to deny it, but was caught by the artless good humour in her expression, and instead said with a smile:

'Perhaps a little at first—just from surprise, you know. But I would not have you think me unfeeling. I assure you I was sincerely concerned at your plight.'

'Well, I am very glad you chose to walk down the lane at the time you did, for had you not, I might still be there now. I beg your pardon—I believe I was so confused that I forgot to thank you.'

He waved away her thanks and then conversation was at an end for a few moments as they attended to the dance.

'Is that your sister, dancing with Mr. Wilcox?' said Maria, when they were once again at liberty to converse, then, as he assented, 'How fine she is! And who is that gentleman near them, dancing with Mary?'

'That is my friend Sands,' said Mr. Fairhead. 'He is staying at Netherfield with us at present. I have not known him long. We met a year ago and took a liking to one another. He is much cleverer than I, especially in the matter of the stocks.'

'I am glad that such things are left to men,' said Maria. 'I know nothing of stocks.'

'Nor do I,' he said with a smile. 'But Sands is wild about them, and fancies himself an expert. He has been talking of a scheme of his to invest in some certificates in India in the eight per cents. I should not touch it myself, for I never understand such things, but he is going all in, and, I have no doubt, will do very well out of it.'

There was little more to be said on a subject about which neither of them knew anything, and so they fell silent again.

'How pleasant it is to have new people here,' said Maria after a few minutes. 'I love my home, but I confess that the time passes slowly sometimes. Your arrival has caused a great deal of excitement in the neighbourhood.'

'I fear we are but plain, dull people, and will not justify anybody's excitement,' said Mr. Fairhead. 'My father in particular brought us here because he was tired of the noise and bustle of London, and was anxious to live in the country.'

'Oh, I am sure you cannot be plain and dull if you bring news of London with you. Although, of course, a gentleman cannot give news of the latest fashions.'

'No. You had better ask my sister about that, for I fear I could not do the justice to the subject which it deserves —unless you would be content with my telling you that such and such a dress was red, or such and such another blue.'

'Oh! No, that would not do at all,' said Maria with a laugh. 'Then you need not fear my asking you about it.'

They continued down the dance, each very pleased with the other as a partner. Maria thought how agreeable it was to dance with such a handsome gentleman who had such beautiful manners, while Thomas Fairhead admired Maria's artlessness and clear complexion, and was relieved that she did not seem to be at pains to demonstrate more wit than he was able to understand—for he was a young man of simple tastes at heart, and too much clever repartee puzzled him. He felt a little regret that Miss Lucas seemed to have been spoken for by Mr. Thripp, but he was a philosophical man and determined not to let himself be downcast by it. There was no harm in enjoying her company for a few minutes at a ball, and presumably she knew what she was about and would not encourage any attentions she was not permitted to accept. Without looking any further, Mr. Fairhead was pleased that he had obeyed his father's wishes and come to the assembly that evening, and felt that perhaps life in the country might turn out to be pleasanter than he had anticipated.

CHAPTER 7

Meanwhile, Miss King had two causes for vexation. The first and most immediate one was Mr. Sands, who *would* detain her with his idle prattle following their dance. Would he only have limited his observations to the ball and other general matters, she would have minded it less, but he was at present engaged in a lengthy and minute description of some transaction in which he had doubled his income, bested a friend of his, and proved beyond doubt his superior judgment in all things. Mary was listening with only half an ear, and did not understand above a quarter of what he was saying, but she was forced to smile and appear interested—an ordinary display of manners which he chose to take as encouragement to begin the story over again once he had finished it. Mary's second cause for vexation was the sight of Maria Lucas and Thomas Fairhead, standing not ten feet away, laughing together. Mary knew not how Maria had succeeded in detaining Mr. Fairhead after the dance, but the sight irritated her, for she felt that their positions ought to be exchanged, and that *Maria* ought to be the one standing with Mr. Sands and listening to his nonsense, so allowing Mary to continue with her scheme to draw in Thomas Fairhead.

At last, to her relief, she was rescued by Sir William, who had overheard something of what Mr. Sands was saying and wanted to hear the story over again. Mary might have chosen that moment to escape, but instead she was struck by an idea, for she had just seen Mr. Thripp approach Maria and Thomas Fairhead and enter into conversation with them, and so instead she remained where she was. Mr. Sands finished his story and went to look for someone else who had not yet heard it, and Mary immediately took the opportunity of saying to Sir William:

'What a pleasant ball we are having, Sir William! I declare there is nothing like dancing to swell the heart and lift the spirits. You see, even Mr. Thripp is enjoying himself as much as anybody. I have often pitied him, for he is such a good man, and his sermons are quite inspiring, and yet how lonely he must be!'

'Do you think so?' said Sir William, who had never given the matter much thought before.

'Why, yes, of course. Do not you agree? All men and women must be lonely who have never married, and Mr. Thripp is sadly a little past the age at which he might easily find a wife, for who would think of him for their daughters? And yet he is hardly forty, and with a little more care for himself might almost be called handsome.'

This was an exaggeration at best, for Mr. Thripp inclined towards the stout, and had long been resigned to the gradual disappearance of his hair, but Sir William was not the doubting sort, and was only too happy to agree with anything a fair young lady might tell him.

'However, I have lately begun to hope that he might find a woman worthy of him,' continued Mary slyly. 'Sir William, you know I am the last one to gossip, but I wonder whether you are quite aware of what people have been talking about this evening. I think it only fair that you be told, for it affects your daughter directly.'

'What do you mean?' said Sir William in surprise.

'Do not you know?' said Mary, directing an arch glance towards the little group wherein stood Maria, Mr. Thripp and Thomas Fairhead. Mr. Thripp was at that moment addressing Maria earnestly, while Maria was flushed and bright-eyed and seemed not unwilling to listen. 'I have for some time suspected that Mr. Thripp harbours a secret admiration of which he dares not speak for fear of your anger. Naturally, I should not have revealed his secret for the world, except that it seems now that other people have begun to notice it and talk.'

'Indeed!' said Sir William. 'But are you quite sure of this?'

'Oh, yes,' Mary assured him. 'Have you never noticed how he sighs after her whenever he sees her? Think, Sir William: has there been any occasion on which he has visited Lucas Lodge and seemed unwilling to leave? I think I need not tell you the reason.'

Mr. Thripp had a great love of other people's hospitality, and especially their port wine, and so Sir William had no difficulty in remembering a number of occasions on which Mr. Thripp had outstayed his welcome.

'And do not you remember how he complimented her looks once to Mrs. Philips? Ah—perhaps you were not there, but I certainly heard him speak of her as a pretty girl.'

Here Mary was not straying *too* far into falsehood, for Mr. Thripp was apt to describe all young ladies as pretty whenever he believed it required of him. But it was not in Sir William's nature to suspect a ruse, and he now began to consider the information Mary had given him with some interest.

'You think he admires Maria, then?' he said in wonder.

'I am certain of it,' said Mary. 'But the question is, does she admire *him*? I know her to be a dutiful daughter, and I am sure that she would never intentionally permit herself to engage her affections in such a way as to provoke your disapproval, but I also know you to be the kindest of fathers—she has told me so herself. That being so, what do *you* think of it, Sir William?'

Since Sir William had thought nothing of it at all until that very moment, he knew not how to reply. He made some answer, then bowed and moved away, and Mary was left to reflect in satisfaction on her evening's work, for she shortly afterwards saw him speaking to Lady Lucas, who looked surprised and immediately directed a sharp glance across the room, towards where Maria was standing. The idea had been planted in their heads, and while Mary could not say whether it would take root, she felt that by directing the Lucases' attention away from the Fairheads and towards Mr. Thripp, she had placed another obstacle in the way of Maria and cleared the path further towards attaining her own ends.

CHAPTER 8

Sir William was not a man of great intellect or discernment, but once an idea had been put into his head he was fortunate by his position to have sufficient leisure time to give it all the consideration it required. Miss King's information that Mr. Thripp admired Maria had caught him wholly by surprise, and he lost no time in taking the news to his wife and asking whether she had heard anything of it, for it struck him as the sort of matter on which women had a much greater quickness of perception than men—although he should not have expected Lady Lucas to keep it from him if she *did* have any idea of it. As it happened, Lady Lucas was as unsuspecting as himself, and received the information with astonishment—an astonishment which, however, was soon replaced by a flurry of possibilities in her mind as she looked across the ball-room and observed Mr. Thripp speaking with animation to her daughter. It had never occurred to her before, but there *did* seem to be a slight particularity of manner, at least on the gentleman's side.

Maria, for her part, seemed much as usual—although perhaps that was because Mr. Thomas Fairhead was part of their little group, for she was undoubtedly too modest a girl to reveal her true feelings before a third. Sir William and Lady Lucas looked at each other and began to consider Maria's future with more interest than they had done in recent years, for they had given up expecting that their second daughter would ever marry. After their eldest daughter's advantageous marriage to Mr. Collins, they had hoped that their son-in-law might introduce a curate or two to their circle, one of whom might do for Maria (for it was not to be supposed that she would ever marry so greatly as Charlotte), but their hopes had been disappointed, and they had fallen quite into the habit of forgetting that they had two daughters still to be disposed of. Now, however, it occurred to them that perhaps they had looked too far afield in their search. Might not it be the case that there was a perfectly good prospect for Maria here at home? To be sure, Mr. Thripp was one and forty, and somewhat ill-favoured in appearance, but he lived comfortably and respectably, and there was no reason to suppose him incapable of making any woman happy if he chose. And so, in the breasts of the Lucases there began to dawn a hope that had never been there before. True, until that moment they had had no interest in Mr. Thripp as a possible husband for their daughter— and there is no doubt that their wish to see Maria married had encouraged them to believe Mary King's information, but the more they considered it, the more they wondered why they had never thought of it before. Mary had planted her lie in fertile ground.

'You must speak to him, my dear,' said Lady Lucas the

day after the assembly. 'If he means to marry Maria then we must bring him to the point.'

'Very well,' said Sir William. 'I shall make some excuse to see him and ask him his intentions.'

Accordingly, that very day Sir William set out on his quest, although he hardly knew how to introduce the subject, since no hint had been given on either side that he might use to illustrate his point, and he could only hope that Mr. Thripp would show no unwillingness to talk of the matter. Somewhat to Sir William's relief (for he had not relished the thought of questioning the man in his own house), he met Mr. Thripp in the lane outside the parsonage. Mr. Thripp greeted him with every appearance of pleasure—for he was going into Meryton, he said, but had been intending to call on the Lucases afterwards. This boded well, and Sir William felt encouraged, and so he turned back and they walked into Meryton together. At first, the conversation remained on general topics, but at length Mr. Thripp began to talk of the assembly and his fondness for dancing.

'Ah, yes,' said Sir William, who saw an opening. 'You danced with Maria, did not you?'

'Indeed I did, sir,' said Mr. Thripp, 'and I hope she was not disappointed with her choice of partner.'

'Not at all,' said Sir William. 'Quite the contrary. In fact, I believe I heard her complimenting your dancing to Miss King afterwards.'

In truth, Sir William was not wholly certain that the remark he had overheard from his daughter referred to Mr. Thripp or not, but it suited him to believe so at that moment. It pleased Mr. Thripp, who despite his heaviness of body piqued himself on his lightness of foot. He puffed up a little.

'Did she?' he said. 'That was like her kindness. I confess I *did* put an especial effort into my steps, for the Fairheads were there, and I hoped to make a good impression by showing them that, while our assemblies are not as gay or as fashionable as those in London, we can at the very least boast a little society which is adept in the art of the dance. Well, well—and so Miss Lucas praised my dancing, did she? Far be it from me to flatter, but I certainly might return the compliment by confessing my belief that as partners we are exceedingly well matched. Miss Lucas is quite as graceful as myself, and any man who is so fortunate as to stand up with her must consider himself blessed indeed!'

He had made the remark purely for form's sake, but Sir William immediately seized upon it as confirmation of what Mary King had told him. He coughed.

'I am glad you mentioned it,' he began, 'for there is something I particularly wanted to speak to you about. Perhaps you are unaware that there have been rumours— indeed, I can hardly suppose that it was your deliberate intention to give rise to talk that might harm my daughter, but you know how people will at times attach more significance to a glance or a gesture than it wholly deserves. However, where there is a risk to reputation, I should be failing in my duty were I not to speak to you about it.'

Mr. Thripp was at a loss to understand what Sir William was referring to, and he said so politely.

'Then the talk has not reached you?' said Sir William.

'That is good. Perhaps it is not known by everybody, and we may yet keep it to within our little circle.'

'Pardon me, Sir William, but if there is malicious gossip going on here in the parish then I beg you would let me know of it, for it is my duty as a clergyman to put a stop to any such evil.'

'No, no, I assure you it is nothing of the kind,' said Sir William. 'There is nothing malicious in it, but I fear that tongues have begun wagging about your intentions with respect to my daughter. Lady Lucas and I are not the sort of parents to interfere with the affairs of our children— Maria well understands her duty, Mr. Thripp, and I know she would never give her heart away in such a manner as to disappoint or disadvantage her family—but naturally, such secrets cannot be kept forever, and so I came this morning to find out the truth of the matter for myself— on the friendliest terms, you understand. I would not have you think that I am in any way angry about it.'

Mr. Thripp was astonished.

'Why, I—' he began, then stopped in confusion. 'I beg your pardon, Sir William, I fear I may not have under- stood you correctly. Can it be that people have been saying that I—that your daughter—'

He stopped, for he knew not how to finish.

'It appears so,' said Sir William. 'I was informed of it myself only last night. Did you know anything of it?'

'Upon my word, I knew nothing at all,' said Mr. Thripp.

'And can you say there is no foundation for the rumour?'

Mr. Thripp did not answer for a moment, for he was thinking hard. He had been a single man for many years, and had expected to remain so. He was well provided for, although by no means rich, and lived a life of ease in his parsonage, where he was looked after by an excellent woman who served as both cook and housekeeper. Had an opportunity for marriage ever come his way, it is possible that he might have taken it for the sake of convenience, but as it happened, he had been saved by his looks from the burden of being sighed over by the ladies, and so had resigned himself with little regret to a life alone, in which he was able to please himself in his domestic arrangements without having to defer to anyone else. Lately, however, an event had occurred which had thrown a shadow over his comfortable existence and caused him no little alarm: Mrs. Partridge, his housekeeper, had, in the summer, been struck down by an attack of rheumatic fever from which it had taken her some time to recover, and even now, several months later, she was still a little weak from it. She had a son who lived in Bedfordshire, and this son had begun to talk of bringing her to live with him, for as he said, he did not wish to see his mother working through age and infirmity when she might so easily come and live with him and his family, where she would be well cared for. Mrs. Partridge would not hear of it at first, but lately, since the weather had turned damp and cold, she had begun to talk wistfully of moving to Bedfordshire one day. Mr. Thripp saw that the idea had been put into her head, and was fearful that *one day* would at length become *very soon*, and then he knew there would be no more comfortable life for him, for how could he find such another who understood him so well?

But now it appeared that Providence had thrown an opportunity in his way, and his surprise was great. He knew not what had given rise to the rumour of which Sir William had just told him, but he could only assume that it had originated on the lady's side, for he was certain he had never shown any particularity of manner towards *her*. It appeared that Sir William and Lady Lucas had no objection to the match, however, and the more he thought about it, the more it seemed the very thing designed to save him from any future disruption to his domestic comforts. To be sure, the Lucases had no money and Miss Lucas no fortune, but Mr. Thripp supposed young ladies did not eat very much, and imagined that two people might be fed just as cheaply as one. He had never thought to inquire into Maria's housekeeping abilities, but he seemed to remember from various remarks of Lady Lucas that her daughters had all been brought up to know what they were about in the kitchen, and he trusted that Miss Lucas might take over from Mrs. Partridge with little deficiency. Above all, however, was one very great advantage, in the shape of Sir William's son-in-law, Mr. Collins, and Mr. Collins's great patroness, Lady Catherine de Bourgh. Who knew how many favours she had it in her power to bestow? Once she had advanced Mr. Collins as far as he could go in the church, perhaps she might have some beneficence to spare for Mrs. Collins's family—and Mr. Thripp, as a diligent clergyman, had no objection to being the recipient of it.

He now saw that Sir William was expecting an answer, and made a show of hesitation.

'I beg you will excuse me from answering your question, Sir William,' he said at last, 'and not for any lack of respect towards yourself—oh, no, on the contrary, I make a point of being guided by your example on every occasion. However, it would be ungentlemanlike of me to speak plainly on the subject to which you allude without your first having ascertained from your daughter whether such an action would be welcome to her.'

He was rather pleased with his reply, since it committed him to nothing and at the same time hinted strongly that the story was true.

'I have not yet spoken to Maria,' said Sir William, 'since I did not wish to expose her to embarrassment if it were to prove that the rumour had no basis in fact. I shall do so as soon as possible, however. I applaud your delicacy, Mr. Thripp, and wish that you might always remain so discreet, at least until everything is out in the open and there is no longer any need to maintain secrecy—as a parent, you understand, I would wish it. I will speak to Maria at once. I should not be at all surprised to find that she has kept quiet out of delicacy, for she is a modest girl and not the sort to presume upon her feelings being returned without receiving confirmation of it from persons of clearer sight and judgment than herself.'

Mr. Thripp assured Sir William that he would say nothing until things had been brought to a conclusion, and the two men parted—Mr. Thripp to consider the new possibility which now lay before him, and to try and begin to think of Maria with affection, since he had evidently and unknowingly inspired such an affection in her, and Sir William happy in the knowledge that he and Mr. Thripp had reached a perfect understanding, and that he might soon be able to boast of having disposed of *two* daughters to advantage.

CHAPTER 9

On the very same morning on which Sir William confronted Mr. Thripp about his intentions with regard to Maria, Miss Lucas herself went out to walk, and on her way back accidentally encountered Thomas Fairhead in the lane from which he had rescued her only a few days before. The waters were now much subsided, and the road was quite passable, but still he shook his head when he saw her, and chided her with good humour for venturing forth after her misadventure of the other day. He could not think of letting her go on alone, he said, for who knew whether another dangerous puddle might not lie ahead?—and it were as well that he be there to prevent her from becoming stranded once again. Miss Lucas made no objection, and they walked together as far as Lucas Lodge, whereupon they parted and Maria went indoors in a state of some happy agitation. She entered the drawing-room, and there found her mother and father sitting apparently engaged in serious discussion.

'Ah, Maria,' said Sir William. 'I am glad you are come

back, for your mother and I have something about which we would speak to you. Who was that person with whom I saw you just now?'

'Mr. Thomas Fairhead,' replied Maria. 'He was kind enough to walk with me some of the way home, for he said it was too muddy for me to be out alone.'

'He was quite right,' said Lady Lucas. 'I have told you before, Maria, about your foolish insistence upon going out in all weathers, and you see, Mr. Fairhead agrees with me.'

Maria was about to reply when Sir William said:

'It is not to be expected that a young girl will have the sense of her mother, Lady Lucas. However, we might hope that when she has gained a little more knowledge and experience of the world, Maria will become quite as wise as you and I. Think, my dear, how far off that day seemed, only yesterday! And yet circumstances can change in practically an instant, as we have now discovered.'

Here Sir William and Lady Lucas both directed a significant glance at Maria, who knew not what to say in reply.

'Has something happened?' she said.

'Indeed it has,' replied Sir William, 'and I believe you can guess what it is. I have been speaking with a certain gentleman—one with whom you yourself have been in company very recently—who informed me most honestly and openly of his affection and intentions with regard to yourself. Do not fear, Maria; I shall not embarrass you by mentioning his name directly—only let me say that it is certainly well known to you, and that you need have no concern that Lady Lucas and I disapprove of the match in any way. On the contrary, although the news has come as a surprise to us both, we are far from inclined to forbid it, since you must be aware that offers of this sort do not come along every day, and the gentleman in question is of excellent fortune and standing in the neighbourhood. Naturally, our fondness for you will prevent either of us from attempting to persuade you against your will, or insisting you accept his hand before you are quite ready. Courtship must move at its own pace, and we would not wish you to marry a man unless you are quite certain in your mind that you are ready to do so—although I am also certain that you will remember what is due to your family, and behave accordingly.'

Maria coloured and stared in astonishment and confusion, first at one parent, then another, for her first thought was that it was a joke—although they were not the sort to laugh at people in this way, and indeed, their expressions quickly told her that they were perfectly serious. To which gentleman was Sir William referring? Maria knew not what to think, for she could remember receiving no pointed attentions from anyone—unless, of course, by his allusion to a gentleman with whom she had also been in company recently, her father was referring to Thomas Fairhead himself. But she had met Mr. Fairhead for the first time only a few days earlier, and while she could not deny that she found him very agreeable and that he had seemed to like her, she had not the self-assurance to believe for an instant that he had fallen immediately in love with her and was already asking her father for her hand in marriage. From what she had seen of him, she was sure he would have had the good manners to speak about it to *her* first. And yet, who else could it be? Nobody else had shown the slightest sign of admiration. Maria saw that a reply was expected of her, but her astonishment and uncertainty were such that she, too, felt unequal to mentioning the gentleman in question by name.

'I am a little surprised, sir,' she began in some embarrassment. 'I had no idea that he had advanced so far in his affections as to speak to you about it—for he has certainly said nothing to me.'

'That is like your modesty,' said Sir William, 'and I am happy for it. But no-one, on seeing the two of you dancing together last night, could have failed to perceive his attentions, for they were quite marked.'

Maria thought about her dance with Thomas Fairhead. Had he, then, paid her attentions? His manner had been friendly and obliging, but she could not in all honesty say that she had noticed anything beyond general complaisance. But if her father had noticed it, and if things had got so far as for Mr. Fairhead to speak to him about it, then she could only suppose that everyone else was right, and that she herself had been particularly unobservant. The idea made her uncomfortable, and she knew not how to look.

Sir William waved his hand at the sight of her confusion.

'Do not discompose yourself,' he said. 'Far be it from me to inquire into all those little glances and gestures which demonstrate a gentleman's feelings, and which are so pleasing to the object of his affections. I do not demand that you tell me everything of what has happened—and I dare say there have been many accidental meetings in the lane about which we know nothing—but if he has not spoken, I am certain that his feelings are not unknown to you, for I understand that ladies are generally very quick to see these things. I shall not press you, however, for some things are better left unsaid, and I am quite sure your conduct when in his company is everything that is respectful and unassuming—no, I have no fear on that head. You are a good girl, Maria, and I know that once you are settled you will be every bit as happy and respectable as your sister Charlotte. Very well; let us say no more on the subject until you wish it. Let it be understood, however, that there can be no objection from your own family—nor, I dare say, from his.'

Maria assented silently, but her thoughts were confused. Sir William's remark about accidental meetings in the lane, which he had made in quite a general way, had confirmed in her mind that he must be referring to Mr. Thomas Fairhead, and she felt a little flutter as she thought of it, for to be sure he *was* very agreeable. But however hard she tried, she could not remember having seen any sign of what was seemingly so obvious to everybody else, and so she resolved that until he spoke for himself, she should make every effort not to appear conscious in his company. She longed to retire to her own room to think in peace about this extraordinary development, but at that moment the younger boys ran in and she was forced to turn her attention to them for the rest of the morning, and it was long before she found the opportunity to escape and reflect on the matter.

CHAPTER 10

Had Miss King known of the conversations which had resulted from her false information, she might have considered the game already won, for she had never dreamed of its having such a happy outcome. However, she knew nothing of it, and since she was capable of great industry whenever she saw a potential benefit to herself, she decided to lose no time in heightening the advantage she had already gained. Accordingly, the morning after the ball, she set out to Netherfield Park to call on Louisa Fairhead, for there had been a half-promise to spend the morning together, which Mary chose to interpret as a definite arrangement. Miss Fairhead was at home, and by no means reluctant to admit her new friend, and the two ladies greeted each other with pleasure, for there was much to talk over, and the ball had afforded many opportunities to compare opinions on new and old acquaintance, and on all the little encounters and events which had occurred the evening before.

'I suppose the gentlemen are gone out,' said Mary with apparent carelessness, shortly after she arrived.

'Yes,' replied Miss Fairhead. 'Or, rather, my brother is out with his dog. Mr. Sands departed for Weybridge this morning.'

'Indeed?' said Mary. 'I understood he was to remain with you some days.'

'I believe he was called home on some urgent business,' said Miss Fairhead, and then seemed inclined to dismiss the subject, for it was impossible to talk truthfully of Mr. Sands without appearing to cast aspersions on her brother's wisdom in his choice of friends.

They sat for a while, then Mary, looking out of the window, said:

'How bright a day it is! I am not one of those who must be out of doors all the time, but it is excessively pleasant outside today, and not cold at all for the time of year. What say you to a walk, Miss Fairhead?'

Miss Fairhead agreed immediately, and they set forth.

'Now, which way shall we go?' said Mary. 'This path seems a little less dirty than the others. How funny if we should meet your brother! I suppose you do not walk together often. I have frequently found that men like to take their long walks across muddy fields and over ditches.'

'That is by no means always the case,' said Louisa. 'Tom is very kind and often walks with me if I ask him, although I do not suppose we will see him today, for he said something about walking in the direction of Lucas Lodge, as he has heard much about the beauties of the countryside thereabouts.'

Mary was disappointed, but said nothing, and the two

ladies set off in the direction of Meryton. On the way they happened to meet Mr. Thripp, who greeted them but had business to attend to and soon passed on. After he had departed, Miss Fairhead observed that he had seemed to enjoy the assembly.

'One does not often see a clergyman take such pleasure in dancing,' she said. 'I wonder he has enough breath for it at his age, for he is not a young man.'

'No,' said Mary, 'but he had a particular reason for enjoyment, in the form of my friend Maria. Perhaps you have not heard, but we expect them to be shortly engaged.'

'Indeed?' said Miss Fairhead in surprise. 'I confess I did not notice anything of intimacy between them—but I expect I was not attending closely, for everyone was so new to me that it would have been beyond my power to observe everything that happened. And do her parents approve? He is rather older than she.'

'I believe the Lucases have no objection,' replied Mary. 'They have little fortune to give her, and they cannot but feel the danger of her remaining forever unmarried, for she is almost five and twenty. Indeed, the whole neighbourhood wishes it, and I have no doubt that all will be brought to a satisfactory conclusion as soon as may be.'

In fact, Miss King had herself begun to think that a marriage between Miss Lucas and Mr. Thripp might be a very good idea. What had begun as a convenient lie to benefit herself, now struck her as a scheme which perhaps would prove to be a good thing for Maria, could it be concluded successfully. She did not suppose it was within her power to force a marriage between two people who had no affection for one another, but Maria was a soft-hearted girl and might be worked on easily enough, while

Mr. Thripp must surely be in want of a wife. Mary made no plans, but resolved to take any opportunity she could to forward the match. It would be pleasant to be able to take the credit for a wedding—and, moreover, would reflect well on her own heart in the eyes of others, for who could doubt but that she wanted only the best for her friend?

Occupied in these happy reflections, Mary walked in silence for some way, until Miss Fairhead laughed at her inattention. At that, Mary awoke from her reverie and remembered what she was about. They were just then entering Meryton, and Miss Fairhead, looking about her, said:

'Why, there is Tom!'

Miss King had no time for more than an exclamation of surprise and pleasure, before they were joined by Thomas Fairhead and his dog.

'I thought you intended to walk towards Lucas Lodge,' said Miss Fairhead.

'So I did,' said Thomas. 'And now I am turning back. Suppose we walk together.'

'But we are just arrived,' said Miss Fairhead.

Miss King here owned that she was rather fatigued after the walk, which had been farther than she thought, and would not object to returning to Netherfield Park immediately, and so Miss Fairhead had no choice but to comply with Mary's wishes out of common politeness, and turn back. Thomas Fairhead offered each lady an arm and the three set off.

'Miss King has been instructing me in the news of the neighbourhood,' said Louisa.

'And I believe I know what that means,' said her

brother good-naturedly. 'It is always so with the ladies. You have been marrying people off—is not that so, Miss King?'

Mary laughed.

'I am afraid you have caught us out, Mr. Fairhead,' she said. 'For what else have we to do but arrange the affairs of our acquaintance?'

'And who is your victim today?'

'I might quarrel with your choice of word,' said Mary with an arch smile. 'There can be no victims in the case—only willing participants. And I believe you know very well about whom we speak, for did not I mention it the other night at the assembly while we were dancing?'

'You mean Miss Lucas and Mr. Thripp, I suppose,' said Mr. Fairhead.

'Yes,' said Mary. 'The very same. It will be a most suitable match for her, for her father has but little, you know, and the Lucas girls are all wild about the church. I dare say you remember, Miss Fairhead, what I told you about her elder sister's marriage to Mr. Collins. The family has done so well out of that profession that it should not surprise me in the slightest to hear that Sir William means for his second daughter to marry into the church too.'

'Then she has not already accepted him?' said Mr. Fairhead. 'I understood you were merely waiting for the announcement.'

'Oh!' said Mary. 'Maria has not confided in me about it, which in itself tells me there must be something in it, for she is one of my intimate friends, and if she is too modest to tell even *me* of it, then you may be certain that there is something of great importance to tell. I dare say

Sir William has instructed all parties to keep it a secret for the present, but I am sure it is a mere matter of form.'

'Pardon me,' said Louisa Fairhead, laughing, 'but this certainty of yours seems to hang upon very little. If silence from all parties on a subject means that something is perforce true, might not we deduce from it, for example, that Mrs. Long is intending to travel to China? For to be sure she has said nothing of it.'

'How droll you are! I am sure Mrs. Long has no intention of travelling to China. Laugh at me if you will, Miss Fairhead, but I will not be shaken in my conviction that we shall shortly hear something of great advantage to Maria—and I shall be the gladdest of all to hear it, for she is a good-hearted creature and I should like to see her happy above all things.'

So the three proceeded on their way towards Netherfield, and Thomas Fairhead was left to reflect in silence on what he had heard, for his sister and Miss King had begun to talk of other things and were now conversing with a degree of wit which he had no hope of matching. He had set out for Lucas Lodge with a half-formed hope— not even admitted to himself—that he might see Miss Lucas while he was out, for at the assembly he had found her company engaging and her conversation undemanding, but there was no-one about and at length he had turned back. He had listened to Miss King's speech about Maria and Mr. Thripp with interest and wondered whether the engagement was quite as certain as Miss King seemed to think, but easy-tempered as he was, he supposed that all things would turn out for the best, and did not mean to discompose himself about it.

CHAPTER 11

Miss King and Miss Fairhead continued very pleased with one another, and Miss King, in particular, was in a state of some complacency about the degree of intimacy which she had reached with Miss Fairhead in only a short time. The two ladies met frequently, and Louisa, who had observed her brother and Miss King in conversation, took care to invite Mary to Netherfield once or twice a week, for a plan had begun to form in her head. She wished her brother to marry, and her friend was the woman she had chosen for him. Mary King was amiable and clever, and would make him a perfect wife, for she had many of the qualities he lacked. In Louisa's opinion, Thomas was too inclined to take the easy path in life, and she wished to see him shine, and who better to help him do it but Miss King?

Had Miss Fairhead known that Mary had got there long before her, and had decided to marry Thomas Fairhead before she had even met him, she might have hesitated, but she was pleased with her scheme, and resolved to try it as soon as the opportunity arose—which it soon did. She and her brother were sitting alone together one day, and talking about marriage, when Thomas said:

'It is a pity, Louisa, that the fine gentlemen are a little thin on the ground here in Hertfordshire, for I should like very much to see you settled.'

'Oh! You need not mind about me,' said Louisa. 'I do not care about marriage.'

'That is what everybody says, up until the moment the engagement is announced.'

'Perhaps. But in my case it is true. I do not say I will *never* marry, but I do not want to fall or be persuaded into marriage merely for the sake of convenience. I should like to marry for love, and so far I have seen no-one hereabouts to whom I should even think of giving my heart.'

'I cannot blame you for your wish,' said Thomas. 'Everyone ought to marry for love, if they can. Well, well, I hope you will soon meet someone and be happy.'

'Thank you. But what about you, Tom? I am not the only single person in this house. You too must marry one day.'

'And I dare say I shall. I do not suppose it is possible to escape it, even if I wished to,' replied Thomas with a laugh.

'And have not you seen any woman here in Hertfordshire whom you might believe capable of capturing your affections?'

'I hardly know,' said Thomas, in a little embarrassment. 'We have been here but a short time, and it is early to be thinking of such things.'

'What say you to Mary King?' said Louisa, for she knew her brother, and knew that it was best to be as direct with him as possible, since he was quite capable of missing even the strongest of hints.

'Mary King?' said Thomas in surprise.

'Yes. Do not you find her agreeable?'

'Why, yes, she is a pleasant enough girl, from what I have seen of her,' said Thomas.

'Her hair is not the fashionable colour, of course, but she is pretty, and clever, and the more I see of her the more I admire her. I believe she would be the very woman to make something of you, Tom. You have yourself confessed that you lack ambition, but I should like as a sister to see you do well in life and be happy, and if you marry judiciously you may manage both. Mary is a doing sort of woman, and she would make you know what you were about.'

'Yes, and so would end all chances of a quiet life,' said Thomas. 'So you have been arranging it all between you, have you?'

'No, not at all,' said Louisa. 'Miss King knows nothing of it, for the thought came to me only yesterday. And yet I do think she might be a suitable wife for you. Her manners are polished and captivating, and she has all the acuity you lack. She has ten thousand pounds, too, so there could be no argument from our parents on *that* head, but I know that kind of thing matters nothing to you.'

'You are right,' said Thomas. 'How I hate all this talk of money when one comes to think of marriage! Our father and mother married for love, when they had but little, and I do not like to be considered a prospect.'

'My dear brother, I do not suppose for a second that Mary King considers you a prospect, as you call it. She is artless enough, and indeed has always declared that she intends never to marry—but if she *were* to change her mind, I have no doubt that she would bring excellent qualities to the marriage, and perhaps that is what you need.'

'I believe she is a little too clever for me,' said Thomas. 'You know I am not one for wit, and I should much prefer a girl who says what she means, instead of dressing up her remarks in puns and bon-mots.'

'You need not worry about that. Miss King is sharp-witted, it is true, but she is also intelligent enough to moderate her conversation to suit. When a woman marries she looks to her husband to guide her in all things, and she will soon learn that it does not do to appear *too* clever if she wants to maintain domestic harmony. I am certain, therefore, that you need not fear her repartee.'

'I dare say you are right, Louisa,' said Thomas smilingly. 'You always are.'

He then went away and Louisa was left to think about what had been said. The conversation had caused her to see the subject in a clearer light—or so she thought—and she was now firmly convinced that what her brother needed was the sort of wife who would guide him gently and kindly towards a more useful life. At present Thomas spent much of his time in idle pursuits—for since the family had left London he had discovered a love of the country, and liked nothing better than to take his dog and go out shooting or fishing, or walking in the lanes around Netherfield—but Louisa was certain that marriage to a woman such as Mary King would do him good and force him to accept his responsibilities. She was certain that his twelve thousand pounds—an unexpected bequest from a distant relative—had made him a little lazy, and it pained her to see him idle his life away without useful result. Fond as she was of her brother, and anxious to act in his best interests, Louisa did not see that her wishes for his future might not align with his own wishes for himself, and although she *said* it was no concern of hers how he chose to dispose of himself, in reality she did not believe him capable of doing what was best, and could not help but try to influence him despite her avowed intention not to interfere.

Thomas, for his part, loved his sister, and although he believed himself capable of acting independently without reference to anyone else, his affection for her meant that he was frequently influenced by her. Accordingly, he reflected on Louisa's words, and wondered whether she might not be right, and whether he ought not to be guided by her in his choice of mate, for he was fully as cognisant as she of his deficiencies—although, unlike Louisa, he was not disturbed by them, and on the contrary had always been secretly glad that he was not so intelligent as to make people expect great things of him, for he much preferred a peaceful life.

Although he had not said as much to his sister, there *was* a woman he had found himself disposed to admire more and more since his arrival—and it was not Miss King. In all their encounters, Maria Lucas had shown herself to be just the sort of girl he liked, for she was uncomplicated and artless, and pleasant to talk to, and gave no sign of having a much greater power of intellect than himself, or of demanding that he accomplish grand deeds in life. The more he knew of her, the greater his disappointment at the knowledge that her affections were engaged elsewhere—for Miss King talked of it frequently, and often spoke of how she liked to drop hints and give encouragement to Mr. Thripp whenever the opportunity arose. Mary could not, she said, be easy in her conscience if she did not do everything in her power to forward the match, which she had no doubt would be accomplished very soon.

Had Miss King but known it, her attempts to draw Thomas Fairhead's attention away from Maria and towards herself had had the opposite effect, for each time she talked of the future marriage between Miss Lucas and Mr. Thripp, she merely turned Thomas's thoughts towards Maria even more—and there is no saying but that he might not have shown his admiration openly, had it not been for the expected engagement. As it was, he had to content himself with talking to Miss Lucas whenever he could—which was not as often as he would have liked —and trusting that something would come along to prevent the marriage at last, although he hardly knew what that might be.

CHAPTER 12

As the weeks went by, Miss King and Miss Fairhead's intimacy advanced. They had early begun to call one another by their Christian names, and they met almost every day at Netherfield Park to while away the rainy hours—for November had arrived and with it a series of squalls. During her visits, Mary took every opportunity to further her acquaintance with Thomas Fairhead, and she was certain that he would be brought to the point at last, although he seemed a little slow in understanding what was expected of him. He was polite and friendly enough, but however hard she tried Mary could discern no softening in his manner towards her. She wanted to believe it was due to his natural shyness and reserve, but was forced to admit that if he did have such qualities then he displayed them before no-one but herself. Perhaps he was not the sort to fall in love very deeply—or perhaps he had a great ability to hide his feelings. Whatever the case, Mary could not foresee any likelihood of receiving a proposal in the near future, and began to ponder ways of encouraging him into action.

Fortunately for her, she soon discovered that Louisa was on her side. They had been talking of Thomas one day while alone together, when Miss Fairhead suddenly said:

'Now, I believe I am about to surprise you with my latest scheme, Mary. Mind, you must promise not to laugh at me when I tell you what it is.'

Mary was all attention.

'Why, I have decided that you and Thomas shall marry,' said Louisa. 'Now, what do you think of that?'

Mary had many thoughts, none of which it was fitting to express before her friend. She hid her triumph and gave an exclamation of surprise.

'What? I, marry your brother?' she said, laughing. 'Why, Louisa, what an odd notion! What on earth made you think of it?'

'You do not immediately say no, I see,' said Louisa archly. 'Then the idea is not unwelcome to you.'

'Now you are teasing me,' said Mary. 'I am only surprised, that is all, for the thought of such a thing had never entered my head. Now, come—you must tell me everything. Has this come from your brother himself? For if it has, then I shall not know how to look the next time I see him.'

'No, the idea springs entirely from my own fancy,' replied Louisa. 'I assure you he has said nothing to me about it. It is only that on seeing the two of you talking and laughing together yesterday, it suddenly came to me that it would be the very thing. Only think, Mary! We should be sisters. Does not it sound a delightful scheme to you?'

'Upon my word, it is a scheme indeed,' said Mary. 'For us to be sisters would please me of all things—but you forget, Louisa, that I have vowed never to marry.'

'That is nothing. I know you better than you think, and I am certain that you made your resolution only because there were no gentlemen in the place agreeable enough to induce you to change your mind. But now— you cannot say Tom is not agreeable. Nobody could possibly think him anything less than perfectly pleasant. I am his sister, and therefore partial, but confess it: do not you find his manners pleasing?'

'Oh! He is beyond comparison the most amiable man of my acquaintance, certainly. But what *I* think does not matter. Whether I find him charming or not, it is not for *me* to speak. That is entirely the prerogative of your brother—and, pardon me, you have said nothing about whether *he* approves of the idea. Even supposing I were to change my mind and declare myself in favour of marriage, it is not simply a case of to speak is to have. Nor will your desire for us to be sisters change anything; it all depends entirely on the whim—or let us say, the inclina-tion—of Mr. Thomas Fairhead.'

'But he admires you, Mary, I am sure he does. To be sure, he is a little uncertain of himself and does not always know what he is about, but I am convinced that he may be *made* to know it. He needs a woman such as yourself— someone clever, who will guide him. Now, do not deny me; think about it, I beg you. The scheme has come as a surprise to you, but I am sure that when you have had time to think about it, you will agree with me that it is a delightful one. I know I shall succeed with you at last.'

Mary laughed and shook her head, and out of seeming modesty turned the subject, but inwardly she was delighted, for she was now certain of an ally in her campaign. She and Louisa between them would work on Thomas Fairhead, and before the year was out she trusted she would be preparing to leave her old name behind her in favour of a new.

CHAPTER 13

Now that Miss King and Miss Fairhead were become the greatest of friends, Maria Lucas found herself left increasingly without company, for it seemed that Mary had no time for her any more, caught up as she was in almost daily visits to Netherfield. When they *did* meet, Mary did nothing but talk in glowing terms of Louisa, and about how they had done such and such a thing or had been to such and such a place. Thomas Fairhead's name was inevitably mentioned often, for it seemed he was frequently in company with them, and Maria longed to be able to confide in Mary and relate to her what Sir William had told her. Her parents had avoided the subject altogether since that day, and she supposed they were keeping their promise to give her time to consider it. She was glad of it, for she had not the courage to speak of it to them—and indeed, was by no means so sanguine about Mr. Fairhead's affection as they seemed to be. The Fairheads had been invited to dine with the Lucases once or twice, and they had all been together at the usual evening-parties, at which, if Mr. Fairhead had wished to speak, he might easily have found the opportunity to do so; but somehow it always seemed to happen that Maria was placed next to Mr. Thripp, who appeared to think it his duty to engage her in conversation to the exclusion of everyone else. He was particularly animated on the subject of her sister, and of Charlotte's happiness in having married a clergyman, and returned to it again and again—with occasional asides in which he declared his conviction that of all professions, the clergy was by far the most respectable and worthy of admiration, and informed her that Sir William himself had stated it to be his firmest opinion that a woman ought to prefer a clergyman over anyone else for a husband. Maria listened to him politely, for he seemed to require no contribution from her beyond the occasional, 'oh, yes,' or 'oh, no,' but she wondered how any man could be quite so devoted to his profession as to have seemingly nothing else to talk about as Mr. Thripp was.

Whenever she managed to escape from Mr. Thripp, she did *sometimes* have the impression that Thomas Fairhead would have liked to speak to her, for he not infrequently drew near enough to begin a conversation; however, at such moments, she was invariably saved from the disadvantage of his seeing her struck dumb with embarrassment in his presence, by the arrival of Miss Fairhead and Mary, who, on each such occasion, would arrive and capture him for themselves. Then she had nothing to do but remain silent and listen to their witticisms, for she could not but admit with an inward sigh that the two of them were much cleverer than she. As she stood in silence, she could not help observing that Miss King seemed to pay Mr. Fairhead a great deal of attention, and this surprised her, for Mary had often spoken of her disdain for men and her resolve never to marry. It was evident that she did not find Mr. Fairhead's company unpleasant, however, and Maria, doubtingly, began to wonder whether Mary were *quite* so determined against marriage as she had always declared herself to be. In addition, she saw that Louisa Fairhead did everything in her power to further all attempts at conversation between her brother and her friend. Maria knew not how to account for this except by supposing that Miss Fairhead was in favour of a match between the two. But how could a sister presume to throw a prospective bride in the way of her brother, if not expressly permitted by him to do so? It seemed to Maria that Mr. Fairhead must have no objection to it, or he would not have allowed her to take such a liberty.

Left to think on the matter, Maria was therefore forced to the conclusion that Thomas Fairhead did *not* admire her, and that Sir William must have been mistaken in what he had heard. But it was strange! Her father was, perhaps, not the cleverest of men, but she had never known him to lose all power of understanding entirely, and he had been quite certain that Mr. Fairhead had declared his affection for her and his wish to marry her. How could he have been so mistaken, in that case? Had Mr. Fairhead perhaps been referring to someone else, when he spoke to her father? It seemed much more likely that if he *had* fallen in love with someone, that that someone was Mary King, for they were thrown together so often in company, and Mary boasted so openly of their intimacy, and seemed so pleased with him, that who else could it be? Yes—that must surely be what had happened: Sir William had come upon Mr. Fairhead and had somehow surprised him into a confession of his love for Mary King. Maria could not say quite how her father had received the impression that Mr. Fairhead had been talking about *her*, but it was the only thing which seemed to make sense. Perhaps Sir William's affection for her had over-ridden all else, and he had been only too happy to interpret Mr. Fairhead's words as referring to Maria. Whatever the case, it was almost certain that Mr. Fairhead cared nothing for her, and that Sir William was wrong.

As soon as she reached this conclusion, Maria felt a sense of relief, for the idea of Thomas Fairhead's having announced his love for her all over Meryton, before she had even begun to think about him in any great degree, had caused her a great deal of disquiet. Now, in the knowledge that they were quite as they had been before, she felt perfectly easy and equal to talking to him again without embarrassment. He need never know what had been said about them, and she could laugh to herself at everybody's lack of perception. To be sure, the idea of his preferring Mary over herself gave her some pain, for she could not deny that she found him very agreeable, but she thought too little of herself to imagine that she had any claims to his attention.

'Mamma has always told me what a foolish creature I am,' she said to herself, 'and it is true enough; I cannot match Mary's wit in conversation, or understand clever remarks, or play the pianoforte, or speak French. I have nothing to set me apart from other young ladies—why, then, should I hope for anything more than I have? I must learn to be happy as I am, and not wish for more, for I am certainly not clever enough to deserve it.'

CHAPTER 14

'You are in good looks today, Maria,' observed Lady Lucas one day in late November. 'Remember that Mr. Thripp is expected to dine this evening. I hope you will wear your new pink silk, for it becomes you very well.'

'Thank you, ma'am,' replied Maria. 'I had not begun to think about it, but I believe I shall do as you advise.'

'You are an obliging girl,' said Lady Lucas, in great good humour, 'and I hope you will continue to show it before Mr. Thripp.'

Maria did not quite understand what Lady Lucas meant, but she was not attending fully, for she was at that moment engaged in threading a needle. Had she been less inclined to retreat into her own thoughts, she might have noticed a particular tone to her mother's voice, and become suspicious. As it was, she suspected nothing, and had no idea that anything particular was intended for that evening except a dinner with her father's friend.

As for Mr. Thripp, he had resolved that this evening

should determine his future, and that by the end of it he should know whether he were to remain a single man or no, for he was becoming impatient. For the first week or two after he had received the hint that Maria Lucas was in love with him, he had taken pains to converse with her and deepen their acquaintance, but according to his observations she seemed much as usual, and at last he was forced to admit to himself that if she *did* harbour an affection for him, she kept it well hidden. It was not to be supposed that Sir William could be mistaken, so Mr. Thripp could only assume from her conduct that she was shyer than he had supposed, and that it would take some time and effort to encourage her to open her heart to him. There was no hurry, however, for in the meantime, Mrs. Partridge had continued to improve in health, and had served up a succession of such delicious dinners that by the end of November he had begun to feel secure. It would be long, he was sure, before he needed to seek her replacement. But alas for all his confidence! Two days ago his housekeeper had fallen ill again, and had taken to her bed, and Mr. Thripp once again foresaw the danger of her permanent removal to Bedfordshire. His comfort must not be attacked, or life would be miserable indeed! He felt the need to settle the matter quickly—regretted having left his future in doubt for so long—and was now determined that there was no time for delicacy, and that Miss Lucas must be persuaded to reveal her true feelings for him as soon as may be.

Accordingly, he arrived at Lucas Lodge in good time, having been more than usually fastidious in dressing, and they all sat down to their meal. Lady Lucas took care to inform Mr. Thripp that Maria had been responsible for the soup, which had turned out particularly well. He turned to Maria and complimented her on her abilities in the kitchen.

'For it is the duty of every woman to understand what she is about in the home,' he said. 'Whether rich or poor, a woman who has been taught nothing of housekeeping ought to be censured; and her mother must bear a large part of the blame for having neglected such an important part of her daughter's education. Lady Lucas is to be commended for having taught you well,' (this with a bow in that lady's direction).

'It was the first wish of my heart that my daughters be taught the domestic arts,' said Lady Lucas. 'I should not have been easy had I seen them grow up without it. I know that *some* families prefer to fill their daughters' heads with pretty accomplishments: music, drawing, and what-not—but what use are those when there are four dozen apples waiting in the kitchen to be put into pies? A concerto is a fine thing, but it will not feed a family, Mr. Thripp, and we cannot all hope that our daughters will marry great gentlemen, and do nothing but sit idly in the drawing-room all day. A woman ought to know how to be useful, and I should have considered myself to be neglecting my duty had I not insisted Maria learn it. She is a good girl, and, I flatter myself, has taken her lessons well. I do not think one could find anything wanting in her.'

'I have no doubt of it,' said Mr. Thripp, with a complacent smile at Miss Lucas.

The gentlemen did not sit long after dinner, for as soon as he had arrived at Lucas Lodge, Mr. Thripp had dropped a hint of his intentions to his host. Sir William was only too happy to oblige, and had apprised Lady Lucas of what they might expect, that she might assist in forwarding their plans. Accordingly, very shortly after the ladies removed to the drawing-room, Sir William sent Mr. Thripp to join them, while he himself retired to his study to await events.

'Maria, my dear,' said Lady Lucas, after the three of them had sat a while. 'I do not believe Mr. Thripp has seen the napkins you embroidered so prettily last week. Perhaps you might fetch them to show him.'

Maria obeyed without question, but when she returned to the drawing-room, she found only Mr. Thripp there.

'Where is Mamma?' she said.

'She was wanted,' he replied. 'I dare say she will be back shortly.'

There followed a short silence, for Mr. Thripp, while not usually uncertain of himself, was unaccustomed to courtship, and was reflecting on how best to proceed so as to be sure of attaining his object. He soon remembered that he was supposed to be admiring Maria's needle-work.

'And so these are the very napkins to which your mother alluded as having been wrought by your own fair hand,' he cried, taking up one of the aforesaid articles and striking an attitude of delight. 'They are quite charming. I congratulate you, Miss Lucas, on the industry and accomplishment which produced so harmonious an object—for this little scrap of fabric I hold here in my hand combines both beauty and utility, and is in every respect a thing to be preserved and cherished.'

Here he paused to congratulate himself inwardly on

having begun so well, for he recalled having heard that to pay compliments was the surest way to win a woman's heart.

'Thank you, sir,' said Maria, in some surprise, for she knew not why her modest handiwork should inspire such a display of ecstasy. 'It was at Mamma's suggestion that I did them.'

'Ah! Your dear mother,' said Mr. Thripp. 'Happy thought indeed! And happy the table that is so fortunate to find itself adorned with such precious works of art!'

Maria wished to reply, but knew not how, for his raptures seemed to her to be so out of proportion to what was required, that she wondered whether he was making fun of her. He *seemed* serious enough, however. Might he, then, be in drink? He had certainly partaken of the wine at dinner with great eagerness. Maria glanced at the door involuntarily and hoped her mother might return soon.

Mr. Thripp was pleased with his beginning, and wished now to press his advantage. It was his object to inform Maria of the advantages which she might expect as his wife, and so he began by talking of his house, and the comfortable arrangements which might be found therein.

'I was only too delighted to accept your dear mother's invitation this evening, Miss Lucas,' he said, 'for in my opinion Lucas Lodge is one of the most charming houses in the neighbourhood, and quite the only one for which I should consider leaving my own fireside of a winter's evening. It is not, perhaps, the thing to say, but I am sure that, as a young woman of feeling, you will understand that there is nothing like the comforts of one's own home.

I do not remember whether you have ever been inside the parsonage?'

'I do not know—that is, I think I have, but when I was quite a child,' said Miss Lucas.

'Ah! Then you will not have seen the changes I have made since I took over the living here in Meryton. That is not to say that I have altered the place out of all recognition—indeed, far be it from me to ruin the associations of *your* childhood, for I should wish that when you return, you will see it quite as you remember it, and that it will awaken many happy memories.'

'Oh! I have no particular memories of it,' said Maria. 'Indeed, I do not think I was ever there above two or three times.'

'All the better!' cried Mr. Thripp. 'Then I trust I need not fear your disapproval if you find I have blocked up a door here, or painted a closet there.'

'By no means,' said Maria.

'It is of the utmost importance to me,' went on Mr. Thripp, 'that the arrangements of my humble home be not unwelcome to those whom I choose to invite into it— I allude especially to the fair sex, naturally, for I know that ladies in general are particularly fastidious in bestowing their approval in these cases.'

'Perhaps they are,' said Maria hesitantly. 'Yes, I believe you are right—it is usually women who care about the looks of a house, while men are commonly supposed to take little notice of such things. I dare say that is because a woman is at home so much more than a man.'

'Indeed, that is the very reason,' said Mr. Thripp. 'And yet a single man is unlike other men, I believe, for he has not a wife to take care of the domestic sphere, and must shift for himself in many ways. Mrs. Partridge is an excellent woman, but she has not the deep interest in the precise colour to be used on the walls of the dining-room as she would be if she were mistress of the house. I had some thought of changing yellow for green, or perhaps a pale blue. What think you, Miss Lucas?'

'I could not say, without seeing it first,' said Maria.

'But what is *your* favourite colour? I believe that with one word from you I should change my mind completely, for I quite look upon you as my guide in all things.'

Here Maria made some general answer as to the advisability of considering the effects of the sunlight at different times of day, but inwardly she was feeling more and more uncomfortable, for by now she was almost certain that Mr. Thripp had taken too much to drink, and she longed for her mother to return and save her from a conversation which she was having some difficulty in following. Mr. Thripp seemed to be dropping hints and allusions to something which she did not understand. Why was *she* to be his guide? Surely if he wanted advice on how to improve his house, he ought to ask her mother, or Mrs. Long, or some other person with knowledge of such things?

Mr. Thripp now caught up one of the napkins and examined it again.

'Ah! Blue!' he said. 'You have embroidered it in blue! I have my answer. Blue it shall be, and these napkins, or just such another set, will take their pride of place on the table as early as may be.'

'I shall be more than happy to work you another set, sir,' said Maria in astonishment. 'But, pardon me, there is no need to paint the room blue to match these particular ones if you do not like it, for I can just as well do them in another colour.'

Mr. Thripp observed Miss Lucas's cheeks, which were pink with confusion, and was certain that she had begun to understand him.

'Well, well, we shall see,' he said. 'I know that whatever you choose, the room will look a thousand times better for it. I trust your taste implicitly, Miss Lucas, and know that you could not make a mistake, for I know it is in your nature to be happy and to make others so, and that you will make every effort in your power to create domestic harmony and accord when that happy day comes on which you will leave Lucas Lodge for a home of your own. I know that Sir William and Lady Lucas are quite of my opinion—indeed, who could doubt that they have every trust in their daughter and her talents?—and so you need not fear their disapproval—although your father tells me that he has already spoken to you on the subject, and that you have reached a good understanding. We must not be too precipitate, naturally—oh, no! That would never do, for we do not wish to provide sport for our neighbours, but I believe we must give them *something* to talk about at last—what say you, Miss Lucas? I am sure you are not unwilling to take my part. Shall we tell Sir William and Lady Lucas that the owner of this fair hand and I are of one mind, and that they might congratulate themselves on the prospect—let us not say, of reducing, but rather of increasing their family by one?'

As he spoke, he had caught hold of her hand, and in her surprise she could hardly listen to what he was saying, nor understand much of his meaning—although it was now very clear to her that he had taken far too much wine, which had caused him to forget himself. She pulled her hand away.

'I beg you would not, sir,' she said, in some agitation. 'Mamma might come in at any second.'

'Ah! Forgive me. I see your modesty does not approve of such displays of feeling—and I cannot blame you for it. On the contrary, perhaps it were as well for a clergyman to avoid them—for it behoves him to set the example for all his neighbours, and it would not do for everybody to conduct themselves in such an unguarded manner, as they might take it upon themselves to do if word were to get out. Yes, yes, you are right, Miss Lucas, and I congratulate you on your delicacy. I cannot consider myself to have chosen ill when you show me so gently and kindly what is right. I wish that every man might choose a wife of such prudence and consideration.'

Here Maria stared, for at last she had begun to understand his meaning, and could hardly believe her ears. What? Could it really be that Mr. Thripp wanted to marry her? It seemed almost impossible, and yet she knew not how else to interpret his words. He had complimented her work, had asked for her advice in the new decoration of his house, had talked of her father's approval, and as though she knew all about it, then finally had taken her hand and talked of a wife. Maria was not quick to catch a hint, but it all seemed to point in only one direction. And yet he had not said the words—had not actually asked her to marry him, and so she was assailed by doubt. It could not be! What? Marry Mr. Thripp, who, she was sure, had never thought of her at all until now? For she was quite certain she had never thought of *him*. Once again she suspected a joke, and in her confusion her only thought was to leave the room as soon as possible.

'I beg your pardon, sir,' she said. 'I have a sudden headache. I will fetch Mamma. Goodbye.'

And with that she ran out of the room. Lady Lucas had been standing by the stairs, and was caught by surprise when her daughter came out and hurried past. She was about to follow Maria when she remembered that their guest was alone in the drawing-room, and went to join him. All was soon explained, and Mr. Thripp had no reason to complain of the progress he had made, although he confessed he was a little surprised at Miss Lucas's hasty departure.

'But I dare say she was overcome by the emotion of the moment, and her natural shyness caused her to seek a means of escape,' he said. 'Perhaps I was too ardent in my declaration, and she has gone away to seek solitude until she can master her overpowering agitation and joy at the happy fate which will soon be hers.'

'But did she accept you, sir?' said Lady Lucas, who could not reconcile his supposition with what she knew of her daughter.

'Not in so many words,' he replied. 'I fear I may have taken her by surprise in my sudden request for her hand —and on reflection, I believe it is only right that she be given a little time to calm herself and reflect upon the matter before she commits herself irrevocably.'

'I do not know how much time she should need,' said Lady Lucas doubtfully, 'and it was shockingly rude of her to run away in that manner. I shall fetch her at once.'

'I beg you would not disturb yourself,' said Mr. Thripp. 'It grows late, and now is perhaps not the time to urge my suit. Let her reflect in private, Lady Lucas, and prepare herself for what she knows must come. As to the eventual outcome, I am sanguine, and do not doubt but that if I am granted another audience with her, then all will be settled. If you and Sir William have no objection, I will call again tomorrow, and I trust that by sunset we shall all be congratulating one another on the prospect of our nearer connection.'

They were then joined by Sir William, and all was explained again. Mr. Thripp took his leave, and Sir William and Lady Lucas were left to stare at each other and wonder at the evening's events. Had Maria accepted Mr. Thripp or not? The gentleman himself seemed to have no doubt of it, but what had he said to frighten Maria away?

'I shall fetch her,' said Lady Lucas at length, and went upstairs to do so, but upon opening her daughter's bedroom door discovered that Maria was already sound asleep.

'No, do not wake her,' said Sir William, on hearing the news. 'Better give her time to sleep and speak to her in the morning.'

Since there was nothing else to be done until Mr. Thripp could address Maria again, they shortly afterwards went to bed.

CHAPTER 15

Lady Lucas had great difficulty in restraining her curiosity at breakfast the next morning. She longed to speak to Maria about exactly what Mr. Thripp had said, and to find out whether they had reached as good an understanding as that gentleman seemed to think. Sir William, too, was eager to know all—although he felt it better to leave the task of finding it out to his wife, for matters of the heart were a woman's province—and, besides, he knew Lady Lucas to be more artful than himself in drawing out secrets. Accordingly, as soon as everyone had finished eating, he summoned the younger Lucases out of the room under some pretence, so that the two ladies might be left alone to talk in peace.

Maria had passed a disturbed night, and had a heaviness of head which she was anxious to relieve by a walk, but before she could announce her intention, Lady Lucas said:

'Well, well, Maria, I confess I am surprised at you. I know it is the fashion to be secretive, but I had not thought you would keep such a thing from your own mother—all the more so, since, if you will remember, your father expressly informed you of his and my approval not a month ago.'

'I beg your pardon, ma'am?' said Maria.

'I am talking of Mr. Thripp, of course! You have not dropped a word of what he said last night. I suppose your head is still full of it all, and you are wondering how much it is proper to tell your parents—and that is quite under-standable. Do not fear my pressing you on the subject, for I should not dream of demanding to know every little thing that happened—no, that shall remain between you and him. However, I think you might at least remember what is due to Sir William and me, for by saying nothing at all you are keeping us in a most agonizing suspense, which is hardly kind. And by the bye, while I think about it, I want also to speak to you about your behaviour in running out of the room like that last night, and leaving Mr. Thripp all alone.'

'I am sorry, Mamma,' said Maria, hanging her head. 'Only, I did not know what he meant, for he was so strange, and you were not there to tell me what to say, so I knew not what else to do.'

'So strange? Why, whatever do you mean?'

'He talked in such a manner, about the napkins, and about the colour of his dining-room, and other things that I did not comprehend, and he behaved altogether so oddly that I thought perhaps he had been taken ill, and so I came running out to look for you,' said Maria. 'What could he mean by it?'

'Bless you, my child! Only to propose marriage! How came you not to understand it?'

'I—I do not know,' said Maria. 'It certainly *seemed* that he might have such a purpose in mind, but he talked about all manner of things except that, and when he took my hand and I came at last to realize his object, I was so astonished I could not think what to do, except that I longed more than anything to escape.'

'That was very rude of you,' said Lady Lucas. 'Why, Maria, I am surprised at you! To have run away in the middle of a proposal from such a person. Why did not you stay and hear him out? You cannot say it came as a surprise to you, for we spoke about it at some length when Mr. Thripp first declared his intentions to Sir William.'

'Oh! I did not think—I understood that—' said Maria, who was now scarlet in the face as she finally realized the egregious error into which she had fallen. It was not Thomas Fairhead who had spoken to her father, but Mr. Thripp! Sir William's delicacy had prevented him from saying the name, and Maria's imagination had done the rest. She blushed anew at her own lack of perception in having initially believed the gentleman in question to be Thomas Fairhead. Had her vanity misled her? No—for she had early concluded from her own observations that although Mr. Fairhead liked her, he was not in love with her, and that if he admired anyone, it must be Mary King. No: she could acquit herself of vanity, she was sure of it. If anything had misled her, it must have been her own wishes, for although the idea of Mr. Fairhead's admiring her had come as a surprise, it had not come as an unwelcome one. How fortunate that she had never had the opportunity to tell Mary of it! It was small comfort to know that no-one else need ever find out about it, and that her embarrassment might remain unknown.

'I have said I should never urge any daughter of mine into marriage against her will,' went on Lady Lucas, 'and I never shall. However, Maria, you must see that here is an unexceptionable match for you. Mr. Thripp is not rich, but he has a clear eight hundred pounds a year, with very likely the prospect of more, if he can but find favour with Lady Catherine de Bourgh through your brother Mr. Collins. Only think what she might do for you if she wished! You are nearly five and twenty now. It is not every woman who has the means to marry well, but here is an opportunity for you if you will only take it. There was a little misunderstanding last night, but I advise you to prepare yourself this morning to meet him more calmly, and to give him a favourable answer when he returns here later to speak to you again.'

'What? He is coming here again?' said Maria in alarm. 'I cannot speak to him! Please, Mamma, do not make me speak to him.'

This was not a propitious beginning, and Lady Lucas was disconcerted, for she had taken Maria's flight from the drawing-room the evening before as a mere fright, caused by her daughter's foolishness, rather than by any disinclination for the proposal itself. But Maria's horrified expression upon hearing that Mr. Thripp was to return did little to reassure Lady Lucas that his second attempt would be any more successful than the first one had been.

'Why, Maria, what would you be about?' she said. 'You must speak to him, for Sir William has already invited him to come today. You cannot mean to say that you do not wish to marry him?'

Maria saw the expression of disappointment on her mother's face, and felt almost ashamed to reply.

'I do not—that is—I cannot speak to him,' she said falteringly.

'Cannot?' said Lady Lucas in some displeasure, and Maria flushed.

'I am sorry, Mamma,' she said. 'It is only that I did not know of it—had not understood that that was what was meant. It has been a very great surprise to me. I beg you would not make me speak to Mr. Thripp—at least, not today, for I do not know what to say to him.'

'You need say nothing,' said Lady Lucas. 'It is for him to talk. All you need do is accept him when he makes the offer.'

'But I cannot,' said Maria. 'I never thought of him before. How can I say yes if I have never thought of him?'

'But do not you like him? Perhaps you are unaware, but there has been some talk about it—and that is another thing, for I do not believe it is right that your parents should have been the last to know about it.'

Maria stared in astonishment and discomfiture.

'I did not know there had been talk,' she said. 'Who has been talking?'

'The whole of Meryton, I hear—which makes it all the worse. Upon my word, Maria, I wish you might not be so unguarded in your manner, for whether you know it or no, everybody expects you to marry Mr. Thripp, and if you refuse him now, we shall all look excessively foolish.'

'Oh!' said Maria, and burst into tears.

'Now, now, do not discompose yourself, my child,' said Lady Lucas. 'Nobody wants to make you unhappy. It is perfectly evident you are not in the state of mind to speak to Mr. Thripp today, so I shall not insist upon it. But you must try and get over this fright of yours and answer him as you ought. The idea of marriage is a new one to you—that much is clear—but I am sure you do not find Mr. Thripp absolutely disagreeable, is not that so?'

'No,' said Maria with a sob. 'He is gentlemanlike, to be sure. But—'

She wished to say that she did not find him agreeable enough to marry him, but dared not, for how could she? It seemed that something in her manner had given rise to the impression that she liked him—although she knew not what that *something* might be, for she had been totally unaware of it herself, and was sure she had not intended it. She could think of nothing to say which would not anger her mother, and so she fell silent.

Lady Lucas thought she understood. They had been too hasty, and Sir William had not explained himself well enough. Maria must be given time to think about it—but not *too* much, for there was every danger that if left to herself, she would never reply at all, and Mr. Thripp would tire of her and go away. A little time, and a little persuasion on the part of her parents, would do every-thing, she was certain.

'Well, well, child,' she said. 'There is no need to cry. I shall tell Sir William that you do not wish to speak to Mr. Thripp today, and he will not insist. I hope you will reflect on your good fortune in having such indulgent parents, for it is not everybody who would act as we have done.'

'Thank you, ma'am,' said Maria in some relief.

'I say you need not speak to him *today*,' went on Lady Lucas, 'but we cannot keep on sending him away forever. Sooner or later you must listen to what he has to say, and

I wish that by the time he speaks again, you might have come to your senses and answer him favourably instead of running off. However, that is for you to decide.'

She then went out to speak to Sir William, and Maria was left to try and calm herself, despite the prospect of having to face another interview with Mr. Thripp soon.

CHAPTER 16

Her headache no better, Miss Lucas soon after breakfast went out for a walk. The weather was fine for the time of year, and Maria felt sorely in need of refreshment for her spirits, so she directed her steps towards her favourite walk, a wooded path which ran along the boundary of Netherfield Park. She was feeling very low after the interview with Lady Lucas, for what she had learned that morning had astounded and shaken her very much. It seemed, from what her mother had said, that everybody in Meryton expected imminently to hear news of an engagement between her and Mr. Thripp, and she was at a loss to explain how this had happened—for she was almost certain that he had given no sign of admiration. To be sure, he *had* seemed inclined to engage her in conversation of late, and had talked much about his prospects and his respectability, but that did not in itself suggest an interest in her—at least, as far as she had always understood from her reading of novels, from which she had found out that a gentleman generally indicated his admiration for a lady by means of sighs and longing glances. Had there been any significant looks? She tried to remember, and at last thought she could recollect one or two occasions on which she had found his gaze upon her. But it had been so little, and so unlike anything that might fairly be supposed to capture the heart of a young woman, that she had given it no thought at all. And yet, it seemed that that was Mr. Thripp's manner of courtship. How could she have failed to see it, since it had apparently been noticed by everybody else? And now, how could she confess to her family that she had no affection for him, when it would disappoint them all so? She would not—could not—marry him, but her refusal would inevitably cause her family pain, and—since everybody in Meryton seemed to know about it—no little mortification.

She was reflecting in this manner and sighing when she arrived at a spot in which the trees thinned and she could see through them into the park. There, just inside the grounds, was a little cottage which she never failed to stop and look at. It had once been the home of the gamekeeper, but its roof had been damaged in a fire some years earlier and never repaired. The gamekeeper had been put elsewhere and the cottage half-forgotten about, for it was in a neglected corner of the park. She turned and bent her steps towards it, and was standing looking at it when the door opened and Thomas Fairhead came out. When he saw her he looked surprised and then pleased, and Maria felt her heart lift.

'I have been exploring to the edges of the park this morning,' he said, after they had exchanged the usual courtesies, 'and I came upon this house, which nobody seems to care about.'

'I have always thought it very pretty,' said Maria. 'It is a pity that nobody has thought to repair it.'

'That is exactly what I think,' said Thomas. 'Why, look —with just a few changes, and a new roof, it would be a delightful house. It is modest, and the aspect is unfavourable, but if only two or three of those trees were to be chopped down, then I think it would be light enough. I should like to live in it myself.'

'But it is not large enough for a gentleman's residence.'

'Not at present, no, but a second parlour might be added to the side here, and I dare say the kitchen might be made bigger. Here is the garden, quite neglected, you see. And *here*, I think a little orchard might be planted, if one cared to wait for twenty years or more. How I should like to sit in the parlour of a summer evening and look out across the park!'

'But do not you prefer Netherfield itself? To be sure, it is much grander.'

'Yes, I like it well enough, but I own it is a little empty and rattling for my tastes. Give me a small, comfortable house with enough room for myself, and perhaps one or two others, and I am happy. Are you walking? Then let me walk with you—or do you prefer to be alone? For you seemed deep in thought just now. But there is a part of the park I should like to show you, from where there is a very pretty view of Lucas Lodge. I do not know whether you have seen it before.'

Miss Lucas was more than happy to walk, and they proceeded together up a small hill, which indeed afforded a delightful view across the country as far as and beyond

Meryton. They spent some time in trying to discern the various landmarks, and then Maria said:

'Is not that your sister and Mary walking together?'

'Yes, I believe it is,' he said, and looked at her. 'I suppose you would like to go after them?'

Maria's spirits, which had begun to rise, sank again, for she had been enjoying her walk and the conversation with Thomas Fairhead, who talked only of things she could understand, and did not make her feel uncomfortable in his presence, or act as though he were joking at her expense. But Mr. Fairhead admired Mary, and so who could be surprised at his wanting to run after her when he saw her out walking? She had no right to keep them apart, and so she assented.

'Then let us go,' he said, and they set off down the hill.

Maria soon saw that he was not walking fast enough to catch them. He had evidently seen it himself, for he said:

'They are going into the house. That is a pity. We shall never catch up to them now. No matter, however. I dare say you will see your friend soon enough. Which way are you going now?'

'What time is it? I had better go home. Mamma will be expecting me soon.'

'Then let me walk with you, for I am going that way myself.'

Maria made no objection, and they bent their steps in the direction of Lucas Lodge. Maria's mind was busy, for an astonishing idea had begun to creep upon her, and she knew not what to think about it, for it seemed to throw only the most flattering light upon herself, which her modest vanity would not allow. Certain it was that Mr.

Fairhead had walked deliberately slowly just now—far too slowly, in fact, to catch up with his sister and Miss King. Had Maria been alone she knew she should have had no trouble at all in reaching them before they entered the house, but Mr. Fairhead had seemed reluctant to speed up his pace, until at last the two ladies had outstripped them. Furthermore, he had directed one or two glances towards her during their walk which, had she been more inclined to trust her own judgment, she would have interpreted as showing a certain degree of admiration—certainly more so than anything she had ever seen in Mr. Thripp. And now she thought she remembered having received one or two similar looks from him in the past. But what did it mean? Whenever they met, he certainly gave every sign of taking pleasure in her company, and appeared interested in her concerns. Did that indicate admiration? It certainly *seemed* as though it did—but since she had already proved herself sadly wrong-headed by failing to notice Mr. Thripp's affection for her, which was apparently so evident to everybody else, she could only assume that once again she had misinterpreted the situation, and that she was mistaken in supposing that Mr. Fairhead's attentions meant anything at all. Why, then, did she feel so fluttered at the idea of being admired by him?

At that moment her own feelings became clear to her all at once, and it suddenly dawned on her that she liked *him* very much indeed! Her astonishment at this discovery was great, for while she had always found him very agreeable, she had thought too little of herself to look beyond that—but now she found she could not *stop* herself from looking beyond it, or from wishing fervently that she might not have been mistaken in her observations that morning. Was she, then, in love with Thomas Fairhead? Her heart, now fully revealed to her, told her that she was. But when had it begun? And how could she have been unaware of it? Her mind was now thrown into confusion as she tried to recollect how it had happened. She could not think of a time when she had not liked him, so perhaps she had fallen in love with him as soon as their very first meeting, when he had rescued her from the muddy lane! It was one extraordinary thought after another, and she now felt embarrassed, for she was suddenly sure he must be able to see everything that was going through her head, and she feared his perception. For a second she was tempted to make some excuse and run away, but after a moment's reflection she mastered her agitation and remained resolutely where she was, although she kept her face turned from him, for she knew her colour was high. In a few minutes she felt stronger and ventured a glance at him. He seemed much as usual and she was relieved.

'I hope your thoughts were pleasant ones,' he said with a smile. 'You seemed so absorbed in them that I did not like to disturb you.'

'Oh! No—that is, yes,' said Maria, more confused than ever, for the events of the past few hours had filled her with wonder and caused no little revolution in her thoughts. In the space of less than a day she had discovered that Thomas Fairhead had *not* confessed an admiration for her and that Mr. Thripp *had*, and then, stranger still, that she herself liked Mr. Fairhead more than she had previously realized, and that perhaps, in spite of the misunderstanding with her father, he liked her too. The whole of it was almost too much to comprehend. The idea of being admired by even one man was surprise enough, but *two* men at once! How could it be? She longed to speak to somebody and confess all, for she feared it was beyond the capabilities of her own mind to understand what had occurred, or to resolve the situation to everybody's advantage, but there was no-one. Mary, she suspected, would not look favourably upon her feelings for Thomas Fairhead, while Lady Lucas, although she would never deliberately make her daughter unhappy, thought only of securing a respectable marriage for her with Mr. Thripp. Charlotte was no use either, for she was certain to take her mother's part. No, this was Maria's dilemma, and she must face it alone.

One thing only was she truly certain of: that as long as there was a Thomas Fairhead in Hertfordshire, still unmarried and still agreeable, she could never think of any other man. This resolution made her feel stronger, and more sure of herself, although she shrank at the thought of having to receive Mr. Thripp's attentions—and still more at the idea of having to explain her apparent obduracy to Sir William and Lady Lucas. How headstrong they would think her! And yet she could not explain her feelings, for she was too well-bred to say that she *disliked* Mr. Thripp, and they would surely not consider the fact that she was not in love with him to be reason enough to refuse him.

They were now approaching Lucas Lodge, and Maria now recollected herself and wished to talk, but her embarrassment had overcome her, and she struggled to find a subject. A similar change seemed to have come over him, for he, too, appeared to be wrapped up in his own thoughts and unwilling or unable to speak. At length she looked up and found his eyes upon her. He looked away, and prodded at the hedgerow with his stick.

'It is a pity we arrived in Hertfordshire so recently,' he said, after a moment. 'Had we come earlier I might have been in time—'

He would not meet her eye, but seemed to want to say more. Maria felt her heart beating rapidly, and silently willed him to go on. They were just then interrupted by a loud tumult in the lane, and saw a group of boys running towards them, who all stopped and yelled at her that she was wanted. Maria's vexation was great, for it seemed to her that, had they been only a minute or two later, Mr. Fairhead might have said something of great interest to them both. But the moment was gone, and could not be retrieved.

'It is my brothers,' said Maria. 'Mamma wants me.'

She bade him goodbye and with a last parting glance went inside, there to spend the rest of the day in agitation, wondering at the revolution in her own heart, and conjecturing as to whether he would wish to continue the conversation when they next saw each other, and what her reply might be if he did.

Miss King, meanwhile, was feeling not a little vexed, for she was becoming frustrated at her lack of success so far in drawing in Thomas Fairhead, who was demonstrating a regrettable inclination to behave as he liked. Mary had spent so much time at Netherfield Park, and had directed so many arch glances and captivating smiles at him—although, at Louisa's suggestion, she had suppressed her natural tendency to lively and sparkling conversation—that by now he ought to have been brought to the point, had he been in the right way of thinking, but instead of submitting to the influence of his sister and the charms of her friend, he remained much the same as ever: cheerful and obliging, but seemingly without any intention of marrying Mary King. And Mary's vexation was become all the greater, because she had begun to suspect him of admiring Maria Lucas: so many times did he come in, having just returned from a walk in which he had happened to bump into Miss Lucas, or mention that he had just then seen Miss Lucas and her father in Meryton, or report some other such accidental meeting, that it almost seemed as though he saw her every time he went out. Only the day before, Mary had been out with Miss Fairhead when she had spied Maria walking with Mr. Fairhead about the grounds of Netherfield Park; instead of coming to join her and Louisa, however, they had kept walking in quite a leisurely fashion, seemingly quite wrapped up in one another, until it was too late for them to catch up, for Louisa had wished to return to the house and Mary had had no choice but to comply. The encounters appeared too frequent to be coincidence—so frequent, in fact, that Mary began to wonder whether Maria were quite as foolish as she seemed, and whether she had perhaps had designs on Thomas Fairhead all along. It had never occurred to Mary that Maria would have the sense to do such a thing, but where there was an advantageous marriage in the case, perhaps she was not so different after all from Charlotte, who had secured Mr. Collins for herself not three days after he had proposed to another woman. The Lucases *seemed* artless enough, but it could not be denied that if there was anything to be had, then they were first to put themselves in the way of getting it. It looked as though Maria were a more serious rival than Mary had at first believed.

This would never do. Mary thought of her ten thousand pounds, which ought to have been enough, and wished it were twenty, for surely *then* she would not be still living with her aunt and uncle, but would have knights and baronets at her command and have merely to choose between them. As it was, her only prospect was Thomas Fairhead, and she meant to have him if she possibly could. But had Maria got there before her? She decided to pay a long overdue visit to Lucas Lodge and see what she could find out. Maria was out when she arrived, but Lady Lucas was sitting alone, with a cold, and was only too happy to see Miss King.

'I thought I should see nobody all morning,' she said. 'It is too unpleasant for me to stir out of doors, but yet I am not unwell enough to remain in bed, so I am glad you are come, Mary. Maria will be back shortly, but I do not expect her to bring any news. We have not seen you here for some time. And so what can you tell me of your aunt and uncle? I hope they continue well.'

Mary replied with such news as she had, but was impatient for Miss Lucas to return, for she wished to speak to Maria in private, to try and ascertain whether she had any deliberate designs on Thomas Fairhead. She had half-forgotten the falsehood she had told about Mr. Thripp, since it had seemingly come to naught, and so she was surprised when Lady Lucas lowered her voice and said:

'By the bye, there is something I wish to speak to you about in confidence. What about this business between Mr. Thripp and Maria?'

Mary coloured slightly, for her first thought was that she was about to be blamed for having started the rumour, but she was relieved when Lady Lucas went on:

'Has Maria talked to you about it? It was you yourself who brought it to Sir William's and my attention, and so it seems I must come to you for information, for to be sure I can get nothing from Maria. She vows she will not speak to him, but speak to him she must, for we cannot leave him without an answer, or he will go away and change his mind about her. Tell me, what think you of his chances?'

'Has he then proposed?' said Mary, in some astonishment.

'Did not she tell you? Yes, he has,' said Lady Lucas, 'but I am afraid he did it in too much of a rush, because Maria ran away.'

Mary stared at Lady Lucas. She had not believed for a moment that Mr. Thripp really admired Maria. Her purpose in telling the lie had been first of all to lead Thomas Fairhead's thoughts away from Miss Lucas, and then afterwards to put the idea into Sir William's head, that he might overlook Mr. Fairhead as a prospect—for Sir William was just the type to try and forward a match between his daughter and Mr. Fairhead if he suspected anything was going on, while Mary's uncle was sadly neglectful in such matters, and Mary felt the need to shift for herself. But now it seemed that she had unwittingly told the truth, and that Mr. Thripp did indeed want to marry Maria. How very strange! It was the most extraordinary coincidence—or so she thought, for she had no idea that it was her own lie which had first set in motion the train of events. Mary marvelled for a moment but, never slow of understanding, she immediately saw the potential benefit to herself, and felt her spirits lift. Perhaps her fortunes were about to turn.

'Then she has not accepted him?' she said.

'No,' replied Lady Lucas. 'You know how easily she takes fright, and I need not say I have remonstrated with her for her foolishness, but we had to send him away without an answer, and now she declares she is too afraid to speak to him again. You must help us, Mary. Tell me, does everybody know about it? Do not spare the truth, for I fear everyone in Meryton is whispering about it and asking what Maria would be about.'

'No—I do not think *everybody* knows of it,' said Mary with apparent hesitation. 'I am sure there must be *some* who have never heard it—and you may be sure, Lady Lucas, that I have always taken great care to deny it whenever it has been repeated to me, and shall continue to do so, for I would not have dear Maria the subject of idle speculation of this kind. It is uncharitable to sport in this way with people's affections—not least those of our friend Mr. Thripp, who must feel the loss of dignity which inevitably occurs when a man is refused by a woman. You will certainly hear no confirmation of the rumour from *me*.'

The fact was, of course, that Mary had never heard the rumour repeated by anyone, for it had sprung entirely from her own imagination, but she thought it better to insinuate that all the neighbourhood were talking of it—first, so that nobody might suspect the part she had played, and second, so that the Lucases would be all the more eager for Maria to accept Mr. Thripp.

'Dear me,' said Lady Lucas, and wrung her hands, for she suspected that Mary had softened the truth a little, and that the Lucases were the talk of the whole town. 'Miss King, you will help us, won't you?'

'Certainly, ma'am, if I can. What is it you wish me to do?'

'Talk to Maria. I fear she is too timid even to be as dutiful as she ought and confess her true feelings to her own mother, but you—you are her intimate friend, and she may say things to you which she would shrink from confessing to her parents.'

'Do you think she loves him, then? For she has said nothing to me.'

'She says she does not, but I cannot find out whether there is any chance that she may grow to love him, for she bursts into tears every time I ask her. You can see the delicacy of our position, for Mr. Thripp is anxious for an answer, but Maria is so very unwilling to speak to him that I do not see how the thing is ever to be resolved.'

'Do you wish them to marry?' said Mary. 'It is certainly a very suitable match for her.'

'That is what we have said to her,' said Lady Lucas. 'I do not want to be accused of forcing my own daughter into a marriage which is disagreeable to her, but really I do not think she could do better. It is a question of persuading *her* of that.'

'Well, I shall try it, if you think I may be of help,' said Mary. 'Of course I cannot ask her to behave contrary to the dictates of her own heart, but perhaps I can make her see reason.'

'That is all I ask,' said Lady Lucas gratefully.

At that moment, Miss Lucas herself came in, and Lady Lucas shortly afterwards left the room. Maria was surprised to see Mary, who had not called for a fortnight or more. Miss King appeared quite unaware of the deficiency, however, and said gaily that it seemed an age since they had met.

'And yet was not it you I saw yesterday in the grounds of Netherfield Park?' she went on. 'I thought I saw you walking with Mr. Thomas Fairhead.'

'Oh! Yes,' said Maria. 'I happened to meet him while I

was out walking, and he was kind enough to show me the view from the top of the hill.'

It was said innocently enough, but there was a consciousness as she spoke which convinced Mary that the danger was real, and that something must be done.

'That was kind of him,' said Mary. 'Why, Maria, I believe he has taken pity on you—just as we all have.'

'What do you mean?' said Maria.

'I did not intend that he should find out about it,' went on Mary, 'but you know how people will talk. I dare say he heard of it from someone in Meryton, for I assure you I have said not a word about it.'

'About what?'

'About you and Mr. Thripp, of course. Why, you must know that there is talk of nothing else in Hertfordshire.'

'What!' cried Maria in horror. 'In Hertfordshire! I had no idea the news had spread so far.'

'Well, perhaps not the whole of Hertfordshire. Do not distress yourself, Maria—you know how I exaggerate at times.'

'But many people are talking of it, you said,' said Maria. 'And Mr. Fairhead—does he know of it too? Oh, gracious me! What must he think of me?'

Had there been any doubt in Mary's mind as to Maria's feelings for Thomas Fairhead, it was now entirely dispelled.

'Do not worry,' she said. 'I do not suppose he thinks of you from one moment to the next, except to pity you, and wish you well, as we all do. But he *did* agree with me that it was a shame that your future has been left in so much doubt through your own want of courage. We talked of it at length yesterday, and he and I are quite of one mind in our wish to see you happily settled. By the bye, it is quite astonishing how similar our minds are! There is such an affinity between us, and he quite laughs at me for it, although of course I chide him for his nonsense. Be that as it may, he thinks you a very good sort of girl, and is convinced that you are the very person to make Mr. Thripp happy.'

'Did he say so?' said Maria falteringly.

'Certainly,' said Mary. 'I believe he was almost minded to mention it to you yesterday when he met you in the park, except that he is far too gentlemanlike to take such a liberty. But Maria, I am quite angry with you. I did not think you would keep such a secret from me—one of your most intimate friends! Can you doubt but that I would have been only too happy to smooth away any little fears and doubts you might have had—done everything in my power to set your mind at rest—encouraged and rejoiced with you?'

Maria hung her head.

'There is no secret,' she said. 'I had never thought about Mr. Thripp until the other day, and I had no idea that he intended any such thing.'

'And yet when I first heard about it, I was by no means surprised,' said Mary. 'I saw you both dancing at the assembly, you remember, and no-one on seeing you together could have doubted his admiration. I am sure you yourself must have been conscious of it, for I am almost certain I saw you blush on more than one occasion. Confess it, Maria: I know how timid you are, and unwilling to think of such things, but I think now you might admit that you were not as surprised as you claim to have been, when he first declared his affection for you.'

Maria was about to deny all knowledge of it, but Mary continued:

'To be truthful, I am very glad of it—not only for your sake, but also for that of your parents. They are excessively kind and indulgent, but you must be aware that it is no little hardship for them to continue to support a woman of almost five and twenty, especially when there are so many other children to care for. Your mother says nothing, but I am sure she must feel it. You know your duty, Maria, and I know that despite your modesty, your sense of right will tell you what you must do. When so many people of greater experience and wisdom expect it of you, how can you presume to know better than they? Naturally, *I* shall never be the one to tell you what to do, but I confess that I shall be very disappointed in you if you do not accept Mr. Thripp's proposal, for I know you well—perhaps better than you know yourself—and I am certain that he is the very man to make you happy. He will show you every courtesy, I am certain of it. And I shall be your first visitor at the parsonage. How envious I shall be!' (Here there was a sigh.) 'I can never hope to be as fortunate as you, Maria. You know my feelings about men and marriage, and I am happier alone, but it means that I must resign myself to never having a home of my own. You must take pity on me, and invite me often, that I might enjoy playing at housekeeping by proxy.'

She had taken Maria's hand as she spoke, and there was such sincerity in her eyes that Maria could not but be deeply affected—not least, because of what Mary had said about Thomas Fairhead. He thought her a good sort of girl, and wanted her to marry Mr. Thripp—so Mary had said. Maria was not the sort to suspect a friend of an untruth, and so she believed it absolutely. This was a blow indeed! Her heart sank, and for a moment she knew not how to support herself, as the conviction came to her that she had deceived herself—or that her own wishes had deceived her. Thomas Fairhead did not admire her—probably did not even think of her, except as his good nature caused him to wish her married to another man. That was the truth of it, and whatever she had believed was wrong.

The happy dream in which she had been wrapped up since yesterday was now revealed as a mere wild fancy. How could she have been so foolish as to think he liked her? It had been a most reprehensible mistake on her part, born of a vanity she had believed herself to be without. Mary King was right: she could not hope to attract the admiration of a Thomas Fairhead. But was it, then, her fate to be married to a Mr. Thripp? It seemed it was not only her parents who thought of the match with approval, and wished for her to accept his hand, for here was Mary, too, emphasizing the advantages of such a marriage.

At that moment Maria felt more unhappy than she ever had before. Was she really such an undutiful daughter as to disappoint her parents by refusing a man who was in every respect such an excellent match for her? Could she really be so ill-bred as to continue to avoid Mr. Thripp, when he wanted nothing but to offer her his hand in an honourable fashion? She was indeed ungrateful if she could forget what was due to her family. They would never force her into a marriage against her will, but she could not wonder at their anxiety to see her settled, for she was now approaching the age at which all hope of ever marrying must be at an end. She knew she ought to rejoice at the offer she had received, but instead she wanted to weep for the one she had *not*. Her pride would not let her do it before Mary, however. She would hide her pain within her own heart, and no-one should ever know how she suffered.

Mary King had been watching Maria closely while all this went through her head, and was satisfied that her words had taken effect. Had Maria entertained any hopes of capturing Thomas Fairhead's heart, they must now have been dashed, and Mary was confident that with a little address, she might soon persuade Miss Lucas that her happiness lay with the church. She rose now to depart, for she judged it better to leave Maria to think over what had happened, but she was determined not to neglect her friend again—at least until she had talked to her enough to attain the object that was now so dear to her heart: to bring about an engagement between Maria Lucas and Mr. Thripp, leaving the way clear for Mary to secure Thomas Fairhead for herself.

True to her resolution, Miss King called on Miss Lucas the very next day, and they walked into Meryton together. On the way back, they parted at the crossroads, with many promises to meet again the next day—although Maria had taken little pleasure in Miss King's company that morning, for Mary had talked of nothing but Mr. Thripp and his proposal, until Maria was quite depressed, and her head was full of the wrong she would do her family and him if she refused him. It was on Monday that he had come to dinner, and she had successfully avoided seeing him on Tuesday and Wednesday through the simple expedient of bursting into tears whenever his name was mentioned. But she knew he could not be avoided forever—and so it proved, thanks to Mary King, who encountered him in the road not a minute after she had left Maria, and sent him after her with an artful hint. Maria heard him calling her name, and her heart began to beat fast as he caught up with her. She stopped and waited in some embarrassment as he fetched his breath and wiped his brow.

'I trust you are much recovered now, Miss Lucas,' he said at last. 'I understand you have been unwell these last two days, so naturally it was not possible for me to pay you the attentions that were due to you.'

'Thank you, I am quite well now,' said Miss Lucas.

'I am very glad, for I have been in agonies since Monday evening, fearing that I may have importuned you to the detriment of your health. Please be assured that such was not my intention; I meant only to show you the utmost respect. However, I am aware that young ladies are frail creatures, and it has since occurred to me that my proposal may have come as too much of a surprise to you, and caused you to take fright. Forgive me if I was too warm in my declaration, but I knew not how to contain my ardour, and I fear it may have been too much for your delicacy.'

Maria shook her head without knowing what she was doing, and wished to be elsewhere, but he had cut off her means of escape, and she could not run away without pushing past him. This she would not do, and so she was forced to hear him out.

'Very well; I can see for myself that you are no longer in any way indisposed,' he went on. 'And that being the case you can have no doubt as to my object in speaking to you now—and for this, I might add, I have the express permission of your father. Your excellent parents, quite understandably, wished to give you time to subdue your agitation and consider the question carefully—for I should be failing in my duty were I to recommend acting precipitately in such matters as these, and I commend you for your circumspection. However, I can no longer contain myself—not the least because tomorrow I am going away, and will not be back until Saturday fortnight, and I should wish for a resolution before I go, that the uncertainty may not weigh upon my mind when I have other, more important things with which to concern myself. I am sure you will not think me unreasonable, therefore, if I allude to the subject again and request an answer from you, for although my affection has not dimmed since Monday, I know you are too generous to try it any further and keep me in suspense any longer, lest the discouragement cause the flame to dwindle and perhaps be extinguished altogether.'

'Sir—' began Maria, but got no further, for she still did not know what to say. Her heart told her to refuse him, for she did not love him, was sure she should never love him, and indeed was very strongly inclined towards another man altogether. But set against the desires of her heart were the demands of interest, good sense, family honour, and the wishes of all her friends. Could she refuse such an unexceptionable offer as this, and live with the reproaches of her father and mother for the rest of her life? For she was sure that only a proposal from a different quarter now would make them forget Mr. Thripp—and such a thing would never happen, however much she wished for it; Mary King's words had made that clear enough. Was the offer from Mr. Thripp, then, her only real chance of marriage? And did she want marriage enough to accept him?

Mr. Thripp now looked about him, to ascertain that

they were quite alone in the lane—for despite his passion he had not forgotten himself entirely—and seized her hand, at the same time fixing a gaze upon her which was meant to be overpowering, for she had shown no sign of running away this time, and so he was certain that the question was all but settled.

'My dear Miss Lucas—Maria,' he said. 'You cannot doubt my feelings for you, or my conviction that our union will only increase the happiness of not only ourselves, but also your family and all our acquaintance. I am only astonished that the idea did not occur to me before—indeed, had your father not mentioned it the other week, I believe I should never have understood my own wishes or concluded that such a thing were even possible, but Sir William's information was the very spur to set me off, and once I had begun there was no doubt as to where I would end. We must thank your father again and again for the happy thought which induced him to convey to me the secret of your heart, for I am sure your natural timidity would never have allowed you to reveal it to me yourself, and had he not told me of it, I should perhaps never have acted as I have done. Only let me say that, despite my slowness of understanding, I am now convinced that we were made for one another, and I look forward to welcoming you to my humble parsonage as my wife very soon. You may be sure that nothing will be wanting, and that any little thing you wish me to do to increase your comfort when you first step over the threshold shall be done. And now, all that remains, my dear Miss Lucas—Maria—is for you to say the word I long most avidly to hear. Say it, and happiness shall be ours before we know it.'

Here he paused, for his long speech had quite put him out of breath again. Maria's first thought when he began it had been to pull her hand away, but his next words had astonished her so much that she quite forgot her intention and left it where it was. What did he mean by his reference to Sir William? For if she had understood correctly, her father himself had told Mr. Thripp that she was in love with him, and it was that which had first given him the idea of proposing to her. But it was impossible! Her father was a good man, and would never tell such an untruth, unless he himself believed it to be true. Maria knew not what to think, and could not help saying:

'Pardon me, sir, but I do not quite understand what you have just said about my father. What exactly did he tell you?'

'Why, he told me of your affection, my dear Maria, and happy for us all that he did, for I should certainly never have discerned it myself.'

'What? Are you quite certain?' said Maria, colouring in dismay, for she had no idea why her father should have done such a thing.

'Quite certain,' said Mr. Thripp. 'Or, at least,' he said, correcting himself, 'that is what I understood by it—and, indeed, he could have had no other meaning. He sought me out particularly to ask me whether the rumour he had heard at the assembly were true, and if it were, to say that he and your mother had no objection to the match. Naturally, I understood immediately what he meant; the mention of a *rumour* was, of course, a mere convention by which he intended to let me know of your innocent affection and their approval of it. You need not be ashamed of it, for you have behaved with the utmost modesty throughout—perhaps *too much* modesty, in fact, for where an affection is kept secret, there is always the danger that it will never be discovered by the very person to whom it is directed. To be sure, it would have been highly improper of you to tell me of it outright—that would have been quite impossible, of course—but there are other ways and means by which a lady may reveal her true feelings: a dropped handkerchief, a glance, a blush—all of these things, if not employed to excess, will convey a woman's thoughts without making her seem forward. But enough! We have been here quite ten minutes, and I fear that we will soon be discovered. Besides, I am expected at church. Now that you are acquainted with my innermost feelings and I with yours, what else have we to wait for? Answer me, I beg you, and put me out of my misery.'

Maria, almost sinking under this latest discovery that her beloved father, Sir William, had apparently been scheming against her, was at a loss to reply. And yet she must say something. She opened her mouth, but before she could speak she heard a whistle, and then the person whom of all people she least wished to see at that moment, Thomas Fairhead, came upon them. He had been chasing his dog, and his appearance was so sudden that they had not time to move apart. The first thing Thomas saw, therefore, was the sight of Mr. Thripp, standing close to Miss Lucas, clasping her hand in his and speaking most earnestly to her, while she listened with the greatest attention.

Which of the three felt the most embarrassed at that moment it would be impossible to say. Each of them went very red in the face, and Mr. Fairhead knew not where to look. Maria immediately snatched her hand away from Mr. Thripp when she saw him, and appeared quite horror-struck, while Mr. Thripp did his best to assume an air of innocence, but succeeded merely in looking foolish. At length, Mr. Fairhead remembered himself so far as to speak.

'I beg your pardon,' he said hurriedly, and without another word, took his dog by the collar and departed as quickly as he had arrived. The interruption had thrown Maria into the greatest state of agitation, and she put her hands to her face.

'Oh, Lord!' she exclaimed. 'What is to become of me? I cannot stay here. I beg you would excuse me, Mr. Thripp.' And with that she ran away as fast as she could, all the way home to Lucas Lodge, there to seek refuge in her room and weep hot tears of dismay, for if her situation had seemed bad before, it seemed absolutely hopeless now. She had still not given Mr. Thripp an answer, but circumstances seemed to be conspiring to ensure that he would attain his object in the end, whether she liked it or not, for the more people who knew of it and wished for the marriage, the less able she felt to refuse him. And of all people to see what had happened, Thomas Fairhead was quite the worst. All hope of *his* affection had now ended, and in the most humiliating way, and she could not but wonder what she had done to be punished so, for it seemed that Fate had lately had no other object than to cause her misery.

Her tears brought on a headache, and she remained in her room and pleaded indisposition to her mother, that she might not be forced to speak to Mr. Thripp again if he decided to continue to urge his suit after his return from church. Her only consolation now was that he was going away for a fortnight. Perhaps something would happen during that time to save her, for she feared she had not the strength or the firmness of purpose to save herself.

It was now that Thomas Fairhead found his affection for Maria Lucas went much further than he had before suspected, for his dismay on discovering her with Mr. Thripp, apparently in the act of accepting his proposal, was considerable. He was not a quick thinker, but he had a methodical and sensible enough mind to conclude, once he had had time to reflect fully, that his discomfiture at what he had seen was due not only to embarrassment—although that had been great—but also to unhappiness at the thought of Miss Lucas's having been claimed by another man. He had long known of the expected engagement between the two, but had chosen not to think about it, telling himself that until it were announced, there was still a chance that the story might not be true—might have been an exaggeration, or a misunderstanding. His hopes had been raised, moreover, by the lady herself, who had seemed to take pleasure in his company, and who had by her looks—he was almost certain of it—given the occasional intimation of deeper feelings. However, Mr. Thripp was always in his mind, and so he had never thought of speaking to her openly until the other day, when they had been walking together through the park. He had been too slow, and the moment had been lost. But now all, all was too late; he had seen Maria and Mr. Thripp in the lane with his own eyes, and there was no doubt of what had been going on. Thomas was left to rue his own idleness and want of resolution, for he was now certain that Maria Lucas was the very sort of woman who would have made him happy, but he had lost his chance, and it could never be regained. The thought brought him quite low for a few days—something which did not escape the attention of his family.

'I wish there were something I might do to help bring you out of these low spirits, Tom,' said Louisa one day shortly afterwards. 'It pains me to see it. I am sure you must be unwell. Our father remarked on it only this morning. He thinks the country air does not agree with you.'

'Does he?' said Thomas. 'Then he is mistaken, for I love the countryside hereabouts, and am only sorry we did not come sooner.'

'But then what is it that ails you?'

'Nothing ails me,' said Thomas uncomfortably, for he had been congratulating himself on having kept his feelings hidden. 'I had not realized that the state of my spirits was the talk of the family. If our father mentions it again I shall be sure and put him right. I am quite happy, Louisa,' he went on, for he saw her disbelieving expression. 'It is only that I do not like to be confined indoors, and all the heavy rain these past few days has prevented me from going out. But today you see the sun has come out again, and I am determined to take my walk.'

'Better stay in, for here is something to cheer you,' said Louisa, who was looking out of the window. 'Mary is come. She will be your medicine. Now, you will not run away, will you? For she is come here in all this mud and you must stay and talk to her.'

Mary King shortly afterwards entered the room in a state of great curiosity, for she knew about the events of Thursday, having seen Maria and induced her to tell the story, albeit unwillingly. Mary, too, had been waiting for the rain to stop, for she was impatient to visit Netherfield and see Thomas Fairhead, to find out whether he had told his sister of what he had seen. Since Mary strongly suspected that he admired Maria, she also longed to know how the sight of Miss Lucas and Mr. Thripp had affected him.

'I am glad you are come, Mary,' said Louisa, 'for Tom and I were just agreeing how dull we have been these past three days with only each other for company.'

'And you think I am the person to bring cheer?' said Mary. 'That is not for *me* to say. However, I shall do my best to brighten the day with what news I have—although there is but one subject on which I can speak, for I confess my mind has been full of my friend Maria Lucas's affairs, and I have been unable to think of anything but her happiness.'

'Oh?' said Miss Fairhead, all attention, and her manner convinced Mary that Thomas had said nothing.

'Yes, Louisa, it has happened at last,' said Mary, with a significant nod. 'Mr. Thripp and Miss Lucas are to be married—that is to say, it is not to be talked of yet, for he is gone away to the North for two weeks, but there is no doubt that when he returns, the announcement will be made, and we may smile and congratulate ourselves on having known of it before anybody else.'

'Depend upon it, you can be sure we will say nothing,' said Louisa, with a glance at her brother, who was listening attentively, as though he wished to know more. 'It is, then, quite certain?'

'Yes; only the date is to be set, and the usual arrangements made. There is always some little problem to be resolved, some little complication to be smoothed away, where a wedding is concerned, but I have no doubt that within a month or two I shall see my dear Maria enter the parsonage as the wife of Mr. Thripp. How I shall miss her! You and I must bear one another company, Louisa, for the housekeeping concerns of a new bride have nothing to do with us, and I dare say Maria will be much too busy to notice us.'

This was another untruth, for Mary knew full well that there was no definite engagement, and that Thomas Fairhead had interrupted them before Maria had given Mr. Thripp his answer. However, she also knew Sir William and Lady Lucas's wishes on the subject of the marriage, and so she was perfectly persuaded that it was become a mere matter of form, of which only the time was in doubt. She now observed Thomas Fairhead closely, and saw that he was low in spirits. This confirmed her in her suspicion that he had liked Maria, and was despondent at having lost her, and she immediately resolved that if a soft voice and a compassionate ear could do anything, she would employ them both to the best of her ability in order to draw Mr. Fairhead's thoughts away from Maria and towards herself. She did not suppose he felt or thought very deeply, and trusted that the task would not be an arduous one, especially since he must now be conscious of the need to forget Maria, and his own efforts would therefore be of unwitting assistance in the scheme. Mary felt all the advantages of the intimacy she had cultivated with his sister, and was cheered by the knowledge that Louisa was as anxious as she was for them to make a match of it. Now all that remained was to win the man himself. She had been unsuccessful up to now because a rival had stood in her way, but now that Maria was safely disposed of in the presumed marriage to Mr. Thripp, there was nothing to prevent Mary from attaining her ends at last.

For the next week, therefore, Miss King—with Louisa's connivance, for Miss Fairhead was still convinced that the scheme to have her friend marry Thomas was her own idea—took care to spend as much time as she possibly could at Netherfield Park, and without knowing quite how, Thomas found himself drawn more and more into company with her, for Louisa was determined to settle the question once and for all, and devised one reason after another to require his presence. And more often than not, Louisa found an excuse once or twice during the day to leave Thomas and Mary alone together.

'He is unhappy about something,' she said to Mary. 'He will not say what it is, but I am sure your gentle compassion is doing him good—far more so than I should do if I tried myself, for I do not know how to cheer him. I see, however, that you know very well how to make him smile, and even laugh sometimes.'

'Oh! I am glad you think so,' said Mary. 'But I say nothing except what comes into my head at the moment. If you think it cheers him, then so much the better, for it pains me to see him unhappy.'

'Then you do care for him a little,' said Louisa.

'As *your* brother, he is almost as a brother to me,' said Mary, 'and I do not like that you be unhappy at his low spirits.'

'Only a brother?' said Louisa. 'Oh, Mary, shall I never then persuade you to think of him in any other way?'

Mary cast her eyes down and tried to blush.

'I do not say—' she began, and hesitated. 'That is, I respect him greatly, and find him very agreeable. No-one, on meeting him, could ever think him anything less, as you must be aware. But you know my vow never to marry, Louisa. How foolish would I seem in the eyes of the world were I to break it!'

'Upon my word,' said Louisa. 'If Thomas likes you and you return his affection, then I should rather say you would be foolish *not* to break it, if he asks you, and I think the world would agree with me entirely!'

'But he has *not* asked me, and so I think we would be well advised not to talk of it so long as it is mere speculation. I am not one of those women who like to boast of their conquests, for I never presume to have made any, and although I cannot deny that I have once or twice discerned certain signs of admiration in your brother, who can say whether they meant anything? Too often we women are inclined to interpret such signs as meaning more than they really do, and while I am not so falsely modest as to deny that a man might perhaps feel an affection for me, neither do I rush to claim that everyone I meet is in love with me.'

'Well, I will not urge you,' said Louisa, 'but if you say you have seen signs of admiration in Thomas then I must believe it, for he is honourable and sincere, and the last man in the world to pretend more than he really feels.'

The conversation then dropped, and Mary was left to reflect on the progress she had made in the affections of Thomas Fairhead—which, she flattered herself, was not small, for she had lately had the happy thought of taking Maria Lucas's behaviour as a model when in his presence. While she herself did not admire the artless type—for to her it seemed too akin to ignorance—it was evident that he did, and so she did her best to affect an ingenuous manner, consoling herself that it need not be for long, and that once his affections were fairly engaged, she could be herself once again.

As for Thomas, he was in the exact frame of mind to appreciate a soft voice and an air of undemanding sympathy, and he soon found that Miss King had a side to her which he had never before suspected her of possessing, for she appeared now to want nothing more than to listen to him and agree with everything he said—quite a contrast to when he had first known her, when she had seemed far too much of a wit for him to feel comfortable in her presence. Gradually, in a shorter time than he might have supposed, he began to admit that he might not be absolutely inconsolable, and that there were other women in Hertfordshire whose company was pleasant enough. He did not wish to fall in love again, but he was not the sort to allow himself to be eaten up with regret, and so he accepted Mary's attentions with no thought beyond forgetting his sorrows by enjoying an hour or two of entertaining converse from a pretty woman.

Mary, meanwhile, was pleased at her success, and began to drop artful hints among her acquaintance about the happy secret which must remain untold *for the present* —for she thought that with a little effort, Thomas's heart might not unreasonably be conquered in the space of a month or two. Within a very few weeks, therefore, the people of Meryton began to talk of having seen Miss King out walking with Mr. Fairhead again, and of having heard from someone *in the know* that Mr. Fairhead admired Miss King; and it was not long before many people were looking forward with pleasurable anticipation to the thought of *two* weddings—for in her haste to spread the rumour of her own impending happiness, Mary had also found herself quite unable to keep the news about Mr. Thripp and Maria Lucas to herself.

Poor Maria, meanwhile, was left to get over her disappointment as best she could, for she had no-one to whom to confide her misery at having found love only to lose it again immediately. Her only consolation lay in the news that Mr. Thripp had fallen ill with pleurisy while staying with his friends, and so his return would be delayed for some weeks—although her relief at his indisposition troubled her conscience greatly and did little to make her more cheerful. Her spirits were not improved by her mother's insistence on relaying to her every little piece of news she heard about Thomas Fairhead and Miss King— for Lady Lucas was exceedingly discomposed at the idea that Mary King should have apparently acted so decisively and quickly in winning the heart of Mr. Fairhead, while her own daughter was still wavering over Mr. Thripp's proposal after more than a month, and could not help telling Maria so repeatedly. Maria, for her part, listened to her mother's reproofs and felt chastened, but could not help entertaining a forlorn hope that the rumours about Mary and Mr. Fairhead were untrue, or had been exaggerated, for if they were true, and if Mr. Fairhead really did intend to marry Mary, she thought she would never be happy again.

CHAPTER 20

Christmas came and went and Mr. Thripp still did not return, for his friends would not hear of his travelling until he was quite recovered. While Sir William and Lady Lucas fretted that Maria had lost her chance, Maria grasped at his continued absence as her only source of consolation, for she had little other reason to rejoice. Mary had once again stopped calling upon her, and the rumours were growing ever stronger that she would soon cease to be Miss King, for Mr. Fairhead the elder had hinted to Mr. Wilcox that he suspected his son of a preference for a young lady, and only wondered why Thomas was so hesitant to speak. He would not interfere, he said, for the young people must be left to themselves in these matters, but there could be no objection to the lady in question. Mr. Wilcox repeated the story to Mrs. Long, who repeated it to Mrs. Philips, and soon Meryton was almost as anxious for the marriage as Miss King could be herself—much to her gratification, for she knew that the expectations of everyone around them could not but work upon him, and she was in great hopes that if he knew the whole of Meryton wished for it, he might be brought to the point at last from sheer obligingness. Maria, meanwhile, sighed at home, and seemed so disconsolate that her mother and father began to wonder whether she were missing the attentions of Mr. Thripp, despite her apparent initial unwillingness. Lady Lucas's spirits began to rise a little, and she listened eagerly to every report of Mr. Thripp's health that reached them, hoping that he might soon return to claim their daughter for his own.

But Fate likes nothing better than to confound expectations, and on seeing which way the wind was blowing she began to work her mischief. So it was that Lady Lucas received a visit shortly after breakfast one day from Mrs. Long, who had come out early with the avowed intention of passing on the news before Mrs. Philips could do it.

'Oh, dear Lady Lucas!' she said. 'Have you heard what has happened at Netherfield Park? 'Tis the most extraordinary thing!'

'What is it?' said Lady Lucas in surprise.

Maria, who was sitting by her mother, coloured, as she immediately thought that Thomas Fairhead must have spoken and been accepted by Mary, but Mrs. Long's next words astounded her.

'Why, only that Mr. Thomas Fairhead has lost all his money!'

'What?' cried Lady Lucas and Maria together.

'Yes, it is quite certain. He lent it to a friend of his, who said he needed it urgently for a personal matter, and then lost every last farthing of it in some ill-advised speculation. It is quite shocking, and his parents are quite beside themselves, for it was his own private fortune and now he has nothing!'

Mrs. Long's intelligence was soon ascertained to be true. Some twelve months before, Thomas Fairhead had been persuaded by his friend Mr. Sands to lend him a large sum, for Mr. Sands had heard of an opportunity which promised to double the money put into it, but was a little short of funds. It was to remain confidential, he told Thomas, for if everyone were to find out about it then the returns would not be nearly so great, but Thomas might join in it if he liked, and of course, Mr. Sands would pay the loan back with interest as soon as the investment came to fruition. Thomas declined with thanks, but if he was wise enough not to put his money into a scheme which he did not understand, he was not so wise in the choice of whom he lent his money to. He had never looked further than his friend's easy assurance and boasts of his own capability, and he took little persuading to lend Mr. Sands a sum which, had his father known of it, would have caused him some consternation, and might have enabled him to prevent the mishap, for he knew of his son's overly trusting nature and would certainly have dissuaded him from the investment.

For the first few months, Thomas had had no cause to regret what he had done, for Mr. Sands assured him that his money was safe, and that there was no doubt of the investment's returning double what had been put in, or even more, and so Thomas was sure of receiving his money very soon; however, he went on, to be absolutely sure of success, just a *little* more money was needed. The company was illiquid, and there had been some slight difficulty in paying out what was owed. It was all perfectly legitimate, but assistance was necessary to put everything in regular train once again. Thomas, unsuspecting, paid what was asked of him once, twice, thrice, and more, confident in his friend's ability, and trusting that he would soon repay the loan.

The date of the first repayment arrived, without any indication from Mr. Sands that he remembered anything about it, although he was staying at Netherfield Park at the time and might have been expected to honour his obligations without being reminded, since there was such a very large sum of money in the balance. However, he said nothing, and so Thomas was forced to remind him gently of it, which ought to have prompted Sands to make the payment—and surely would have done so, had he not been called home on family business that very day. Thomas could not insist upon receiving payment under such circumstances, for the business on which Sands had departed was of an urgent nature; however, he trusted that the money would be forthcoming very soon. By January it was evident that something was amiss, for Thomas had received one excuse after another, and began to worry that Mr. Sands was in difficulties. It was at this moment that the enormity of what he had done began to become clear to him, and he felt ashamed as he realized how little he knew of his friend, and how easily he had been persuaded to part with his money. Thomas said nothing to his family, but each day, when no letter, no cheque arrived, his fears grew, and he began to read the newspapers with more interest than they had ever commanded before, looking for news of the company in which his friend had invested. For two weeks he heard nothing, but at last the intelligence he had dreaded came, when his father, looking up from the newspaper, remarked upon the dreadful calamity which was now being reported, in which hundreds of people had lost their money in an unwise speculation. At that Thomas went deadly white and almost snatched the paper from his father's hands, but there was no need for him to read it, for he already knew what it would say: the venture had collapsed, and with it all hopes that those who had invested in it would ever see a return. Thomas made one last attempt to communicate with Mr. Sands, but received a reply only to the effect that his friend was gone abroad and was not expected back soon. At that, Thomas knew it was all up; there was nothing for it but to confess to his father and hope for the best.

The news that his son had thrown his money away in such a manner came as a great blow to Mr. Fairhead, and for some time he sat there, quite shocked, and unable to speak a word, for it had never occurred to him that Thomas was so little to be trusted with his own fortune, or such easy prey to a plausible scoundrel. Thomas, ashamed and distressed, could say in his own defence only that he had meant well, but he knew he had no other excuse, for he was fully aware that he had been stupid—blind and stupid, and that he did not deserve forgiveness.

When the news was relayed to his mother and sister, he felt worse than before, for his mother's tears tore at his heart, while Louisa's reproachful 'Oh, Tom,' expressed more than a thousand words from anyone else could have. In a fit of contrition, he declared that he would go to London to try and find out what had become of the money, for he was acquainted with some friends of Mr. Sands, who might know something. His father would not hear of him going alone, and insisted upon accompanying him—less out of a desire to be of assistance, than out of a suspicion that his son would not be prevented from throwing good money after bad in his pursuit of reparation, for there was still a small sum left. But their quest proved fruitless; Mr. Sands's friends could not or would not help—indeed, some of them complained that they, too, had lent him money which had not yet been repaid, so there was nothing to be gained from importuning them further. The elder Mr. Fairhead then applied to his friends in the city, who shook their heads when he mentioned the investment, and said they should not have touched it themselves, for there was no doubt it was destined to end badly.

When it became clear that there was nothing to be done, Thomas begged his father's forgiveness, and vowed he would go away, so as not to be a burden upon the family. Mr. Fairhead, who was a sincere Christian at heart, looked at his beloved son's contrite face and evident agony of guilt, and could not but be affected by them. He spoke sternly but compassionately, although by now there was no need to bring home to Thomas the enormity of his mistake, for he was already fully aware of it. There was to be no talk of Thomas's going away. He must come home and they would see what could be done, for at such times as these, it was more necessary than ever to rely upon family for support. Mr. Fairhead could not in all honesty say that he was not disappointed in his son, or that his faith in Thomas's good sense had not been severely shaken, but he would not have it said that he had disowned his own flesh and blood for an error of judgment which had sprung from a spirit of generosity rather than mere selfishness. On hearing this, Thomas felt all the more guilty at having received his father's forgiveness, owned that he had trusted too much in his own perception, where he ought to have looked to others for advice, and promised with all his heart that he would do everything in his power to right the wrong—although what he could do now was doubtful, since there seemed no way of recovering what had been lost.

So Thomas and his father returned home to Netherfield Park, to rest and to think, away from the bustle and noise of London. It had been a hard lesson for Thomas, but his father trusted at least that something might come of it in the form of an improvement in good sense, even if all hope now seemed lost in the matter of the money. Thomas must now acknowledge the fact that his prospects were not what they had been, and that he must moderate his expectations as to his future comfort in life, at least as long as his father was alive—for, in spite of his forgiveness, it was not to be supposed that Mr. Fairhead would be unwise enough to reward his son's foolishness by giving him an independence. No; Thomas had been the author of his own misfortune, and he must now live with it.

CHAPTER 21

Maria had barely got over her wonder and consternation at Thomas Fairhead's misadventure when, to her surprise, she received a visit from Miss King, who greeted her as though their friendship had never been interrupted, and seemed quite as pleased as she had ever been to pass the morning at Lucas Lodge. Maria's astonishment was all the greater when Mary called again the next day, and two days after that, and altogether showed every sign of wishing to restore their friendship to all its former intimacy. Miss King made no mention of Louisa, or of the unfortunate events which had befallen the Fairheads, and Maria knew not how to account for it, for she had been quite certain that Mary would be full of the news and only too ready to speak of it —for did not it affect her too, as the presumed future bride of Thomas Fairhead? Maria dared not ask about Mr. Fairhead himself, and so the subject seemed closed to them, although she longed to know whether he were *very*

despondent, and wished that he might not be made too miserable by what had happened.

'Let us walk out,' said Mary one day when Maria had come to call on her at her aunt and uncle's. 'I am tired of sitting indoors, and you see the sun has nearly melted all the frost.'

Maria had no objection, and the two ladies issued forth. It was a fine day, though cold, and they walked quickly to warm up.

'And so I hear Mr. Thripp is to return on Saturday,' said Mary with an arch smile. 'He has stayed away much longer than we expected, and I confess I feared his illness was more serious than we all believed. It seems, however, that he is quite recovered now, and will not stay away any longer. But you do not need *me* to tell you this, of course, Maria, for I dare say you have much more detailed intelligence than I, and from Mr. Thripp himself. Only let me say that you cannot doubt my joy at your happiness, for happy you must surely be at his return.'

Since Maria was *not* happy at the prospect of Mr. Thripp's return, she made no reply, but merely coloured, allowing Mary to interpret the blush as she chose. Her heart sank, however, for of late she had almost got into the way of forgetting Mr. Thripp and the threat which hung over her head, and the news of his expected return had come as a most unwelcome reminder. She wished to talk of something else, lest Mary disturb her by praising Mr. Thripp for the duration of their walk, and was casting about for a new subject when she suddenly saw Thomas Fairhead, evidently back from London, walking with his sister and approaching them at no great distance. The four young people regarded one another with varying degrees of embarrassment—or, rather, three of them were embarrassed, for Mary appeared quite easy and unconcerned.

'Good morning, Miss Fairhead,' she said, before anybody else could speak. 'I trust you are well. Good morning, Mr. Fairhead. Come, Maria.'

She then prepared to pass on. Her manner was so formal and cold that Maria was bereft of all power of thought, and could do nothing but stand frozen in astonishment. A glance at the Fairheads revealed their surprise and mortification at Miss King's manner, although they said nothing, but merely turned and continued on their way in silence. Maria stood for a second, wishing she might run after them and make some amends for Mary's rudeness, but the moment passed before she could make her decision, and so in some consternation she hurried after Mary. Before she could ask all the questions that were burning in her mind, Mary said calmly:

'I dare say you are wondering at my manner just now. It was quite justified, however, for I have been wickedly deceived in the Fairheads.'

'Deceived!' said Maria.

'Yes,' said Mary. 'Be thankful that you have escaped it, Maria, and that you were not drawn in by them. You were wiser than I.'

'But what can you mean?' said Maria in wonder.

Mary drew herself up.

'Why, that I was foolish enough to notice Miss Fairhead when they first arrived here, and pay her attention. I am not one to boast, but I flatter myself that I am of some consequence in Meryton. However, with that consequence comes a duty—to myself and to others—to act with dignity at all times, and to associate only with those who can elevate it further, for what are we without our reputation? My kindness to the Fairheads has been repaid with nothing but scandal and disgrace, and so of course we cannot remain on the same terms of friendship as before.'

'But surely you do not think they have acted maliciously?' said Maria. 'Mr. Fairhead was too trusting of his friend, that is all. He did nothing wicked, certainly.'

'Perhaps not,' said Mary. 'But there is ingratitude in all this; I feel it. I paid the Fairheads attention on the tacit understanding of good conduct on their part. They have failed in this—or at least, Mr. Thomas Fairhead has failed. Perhaps Louisa was less at fault, but I cannot but think there must have been something wanting from the parents, who have permitted their son to disgrace the family in such a manner, and so who can say what fault Miss Fairhead may be concealing from us? I am not wholly unfeeling—in my heart I long to overlook what has happened, and go on as we were before; however, my regard for myself will not allow it. No, say nothing, Maria,' for she saw that Miss Lucas was about to protest. 'I am upset—I am very upset, and wish only to forget what has happened. You will, I am sure, respect my wishes by refraining from referring to the matter again.'

Maria could not oppose such a wish, and the walk continued in silence. The two ladies were both deep in thought—although their reflections were of very different natures. Mary was resolute in her determination to cut the Fairheads, for she had been sadly disappointed in Thomas Fairhead. Twelve thousand pounds would have been a pretty sum to add to her ten, and throughout the preceding months she had amused herself with thoughts of fine dresses, a household of servants, and the admiration of the neighbourhood. Her own fortune alone would be insufficient to furnish them with those necessities—and she dared not rely on the future, for the elder Mr. Fairhead was a hale, hearty man who threatened to live another twenty years or more. Mary longed for the independence of a marriage to a man of private means, and Thomas Fairhead had seemed to offer that, until he had been foolish enough to place his trust in Mr. Sands. Mary was vexed, for she was almost convinced that there had been some underhanded behaviour—was inclined to suspect, indeed, that her fortune had been an object to Thomas Fairhead all along, even while she considered *his* an object. Had they married, he would have taken her money and given it all to Mr. Sands, she was quite certain of it. As it was, she had had a lucky escape, but now the search must begin again—a melancholy prospect. Mary's face grew peevish, and her thoughts were ones of dissatisfaction.

As for Maria, she felt a lightness of heart which she knew not how to explain. She pitied the Fairheads as much as ever for their worries—and Thomas Fairhead in particular, for she was sure he must be miserable at the disappointment he had caused his family—and yet, when she thought of him free from Mary's attentions, she felt her heart swell with joy. It seemed uncharitable to be happy that Mary had not got him, when Maria could not hope to have him herself—for Mr. Fairhead had no money, and Mr. Thripp's return was imminent—but still she could not help but smile. There was no hope for her and Thomas Fairhead, but now she felt a new resolution strengthen within her, and she felt quite equal at last to refusing Mr. Thripp. She would thank him kindly for the honour he did her, but would say quite decidedly that she did not think they would suit, and then she would resign herself to remaining single. Her mother and father would be disappointed, but it could not be helped.

CHAPTER 22

It was perhaps fortunate that Miss Lucas was never called upon to test her resolution, for there is no saying whether it would have held against the disappointed looks of her parents, and the reproachful remarks of Mr. Thripp. But the necessity never arose, for the very day after she had made the resolution to refuse Mr. Thripp, she met Thomas Fairhead while out on an errand in Meryton for Lady Lucas. He looked at her uncertainly and almost seemed inclined to pass on, and she immediately remembered Mary's cold behaviour of the day before. Had he, then, believed her to be a party to it? She could not expect it of his pride that he should stop and speak to her, so she said nothing, but he immediately said in a low voice:

'Will you not speak to me, Maria? Am I such a disgrace as to have forfeited *your* friendship?'

'Oh! Not for the world!' said Maria, stopping dead, and with those few artless words and a look that no-one could have mistaken, gave away more of her feelings than she

had ever intended. 'I beg your pardon. I did not mean that
—I thought Mary—'

Here she stopped, for she knew not how to excuse
Mary's rudeness.

'I have offended Miss King, it seems,' said Thomas,
'and I am grieved for Louisa's sake, but not nearly as
much as I should be if I thought I had offended *you*.'

'You have not offended me at all,' said Maria. 'I am
only very sorry for what has happened, but I cannot think
it was anything but a mistake. I am sure you did not mean
anything wicked by it—indeed, I know you could not. I
will never believe it of you.'

'Thank you,' he said. 'I have been foolish enough, and
now I must live with the consequences. It is fortunate that
I hurt only myself by my actions, for I should have been
truly miserable had the money been anyone else's but my
own. As it is, I must bear the disappointment of my
parents, who loved me and believed me to be the dutiful
son I ought to have been, and that of my sister, who has
lost a friend by it.'

'I am sure your parents and your sister do not think
the worse of you for what has happened,' said Maria, but
he shook his head.

'They do think the worse of me, and rightly so,' he
said. 'I have squandered a competence that ought to have
allowed me to live comfortably, and have trusted a man of
whom I ought to have been suspicious, for I knew very
little of him. I do not wonder at their censure—although
they have been kinder to me than I deserve.'

Maria's eyes said that she did not believe him to
deserve anything less than kindness, but he did not notice,
for he was looking at the ground. He had turned to walk

with her, and they proceeded together for a little way. He was still looking anywhere but her, and at length he said, with a sort of smile:

'But let us not speak of misery when there is good cheer to be had. I have not yet congratulated you on your future happiness. Let me do so at once, and wish you well, not only on my own behalf, but also on that of my sister.'

Maria had suffered much from her own lack of perception and that of others, but she had sense enough to know that now was the moment to overcome her embarrassment and correct the misapprehension if she were ever to escape it.

'I will not pretend not to understand you,' she replied hesitantly. 'I believe you are talking of Mr. Thripp. I know that certain people expect—but I cannot—could never—'

She stopped in confusion, and Mr. Fairhead looked up with sudden animation, although he said nothing. Maria collected herself and tried again.

'Pardon me, Mr. Fairhead, but I beg that if you were to hear any rumours with regard to myself and the gentleman in question, that you would contradict them at once, for they are wholly untrue and do nothing but cause me pain.'

'Can it be so?' he said in wonder. 'For I have heard talk of it from more than one person, and there was one occasion on which I thought I saw you both—'

Here he hesitated out of embarrassment—and out of pity for Maria, who had turned the brightest shade of pink.

'I do not say there was no wish on his part,' she said at last, after a little struggle. 'But much as I respect Mr. Thripp, I do not want to marry him. I am afraid there has been a very great misunderstanding in that respect, and I am sorry for it, for it has led to expectations on the part of many which—in short, if you would be charitable to both him and me you cannot too soon forget you ever heard of it.'

Thomas looked as though he would like to ask more, but delicacy prevented him, while Maria could hardly say more without appearing an undutiful daughter, for much of her recent misery had been due to her parents' credulity in believing the story.

'If what you say is true, then I must beg your pardon,' he said at last. 'Not for the world would I cause you or him pain, and you may be sure that I will do everything in my power to prevent the rumour from spreading any further.'

'Thank you,' she said.

They walked a little way in silence, then he said, again looking at the ground:

'I will not test your patience by confiding to you all my recent unhappiness, since you can imagine only too well how I have suffered at having disappointed my parents as I have. And yet, strange to tell, I find now that I am not in a state of total misery, as by rights I ought to be.'

'What do you mean?' said Maria, and held her breath, for there was something in his tone that had caught her attention.

'As an honourable man I ought not to speak,' he said, 'and yet somehow I cannot keep silent, even though it is too late now—even though there is no hope at all.'

Here he ventured a look at her, but Maria could say nothing, only listen intently.

'Will it surprise you to hear that what you have just

told me about Mr. Thripp fills me with gladness?' he went on. 'I think it must not. And if things were otherwise—ah, but what use is it to talk in this fashion? I have been responsible for my own misfortune, and I ought to suffer for it.'

So he said, and yet his actions at that moment did not seem those of a man who was inclined to take his punishment, for Maria's eyes were so bright and compassionate, and her willingness to listen to him so evident, that in spite of himself he had turned to her and taken her hand as he spoke. She did not withdraw it and he took courage.

'I should have spoken long ago had I not believed your affections to be otherwise engaged,' he said. 'But now I know you to be free—stay—I have no right to ask it, for I have nothing to offer. It might be many years—'

'I have nothing else to wait for,' said Maria eagerly. Although normally slow to comprehension, she had no trouble in understanding his meaning on *this* occasion, and she felt keenly all the urgency that was required of her at present, if she were ever to be happy. He heard her words, and looked at her with something like dawning hope.

'But you are still young, and might marry well if you chose it,' he said.

'I *do* choose it,' she said. 'I *have* chosen it, and I do not think I could find a better.'

She was surprised at her own boldness, and would have said more, except that a horse could now be heard approaching along the lane, and so she withdrew her hand and turned away from him. The horse and its rider passed, and Thomas immediately took her hand again. Maria felt as though she were in a happy dream, although she knew the way ahead was far from clear. He was equally cognisant of it.

'But Maria, how can I ask for your promise when future events are so uncertain?' he said. 'I am at present quite dependent upon my father, but I will not ask anything of him, for it would be too much of an imposition after what I have done—just as I cannot ask anything of you, for I have nothing to give.'

'I will pledge my faith,' said Maria, 'and ask for nothing in return except yours.'

'How good you are!' he cried, clasping her hand to his breast. 'But are you certain? Think carefully before you speak, for I am but a poor man now, and shall be for many years.'

'I am not afraid of that,' said Maria stoutly. 'Nay, I believe I shall not be afraid of anything if I am with you.'

A joyful smile spread over his face.

'Then I accept the exchange with all my heart,' he said. 'Or, rather, perhaps it had better wait until I have spoken to your father. I fear he will be less happy at the prospect than I am.'

'Oh!' said Maria, who in her happiness had not considered her parents. They believed her the property of Mr. Thripp, and she had no idea how they would take the news of her engagement to Thomas Fairhead—who was commonly thought to be engaged to Mary King. 'My father is a very good man,' she said after a moment's thought, 'and I am sure wishes only to see me happy. I hope he will not make any difficulties.'

'Still, I would not be disrespectful. We must obtain his permission first,' said Thomas. He relinquished her hand with reluctance. 'Here is your hand. I return it to you until such time as it is fitting for me to take it again. I hope it will not be long.'

Here Maria hinted that it might be as well to speak to Sir William at once, since Mr. Thripp was expected to return to Hertfordshire imminently, and so they agreed that he should do it that very day if it were at all possible. They therefore bent their steps towards Lucas Lodge, and Maria did her best to subdue the fluttering of her heart. Her feelings were very mixed. On the one hand she was filled with a most overpowering happiness that at last she and Thomas Fairhead had reached a good understanding, and that all mistakes had been rectified; on the other, she was in a state of trepidation as to what the future might hold—for despite what she had said, she suspected that Thomas was right, and that her father would not look favourably on the match. Moreover, it must be difficult for Sir William and Lady Lucas to give up all idea of welcoming Mr. Thripp as a son—but that was now become absolutely necessary, for whether she were to marry Thomas or no, she could not accept Mr. Thripp as a husband, and she must now steel herself to confess it to her parents.

CHAPTER 23

Sir William's astonishment on being applied to for his second daughter's hand in marriage by Thomas Fairhead was great—so great that at first he knew not how to reply. The Fairheads were a very respectable family, and had things been otherwise, Sir William would have accepted Thomas as a son-in-law with great alacrity, and would only have wondered why he had not considered the young man a prospective husband for his daughter sooner. As it was, however, the story of how Thomas had foolishly allowed himself to be cheated out of his money was known to everyone in Meryton, and could not be lightly dismissed. But it was not simply a case of refusing his consent and having done with it, for there were wider considerations to think of: Sir William did not wish to offend Mr. Fairhead the elder by rejecting the application of Mr. Fairhead the younger; moreover, Thomas Fairhead had been so very open and honest about his mistake, that it was difficult not to take pity on him—for at least it had been due to his own generosity, rather than to any meaner purpose. There was some little money remaining, said Thomas, and he intended to use it to purchase a commission in the army. As an officer he would be posted away from home, and by taking this step might be considered to be doing something useful, while at the same time removing all reminder of himself and his unfortunate adventure from the country. It was his intention, he said, to make amends for his error by living quietly and virtuously, and he wished he might do it with Maria by his side, but if Sir William refused his permission then he would abide by the decision and make no opposition.

Sir William said a few empty words, and at length sent Thomas away, saying that he would have to reflect upon it. But thinking was not something that came easily to Sir William, and he quickly found himself perplexed. For one thing, there was still the matter of Mr. Thripp's proposal to be got over. They had all been expecting that he would come back and that Maria would accept him at last, but from what Thomas Fairhead had said, it seemed she had changed her mind. Unaccountable fickleness! How was he to understand it? He called for Maria, who had been expecting the summons and went along to explain herself, not without some apprehension. It was a surprising interview for Sir William, for in the space of half an hour he discovered, amidst many tears and blushes from his daughter, that Maria did not want to marry Mr. Thripp—nay, that the very thought of it had given her much unhappiness these past two months—and that she loved Thomas Fairhead and was determined to marry him if she had to wait until she were forty to do it. Sir William was much taken aback by such words from his second daughter, who was generally an obliging creature, but he was even more astounded to discover that she believed *him* to have been the instigator of the scheme to marry her to Mr. Thripp. Her sense of duty had prevented her from reproaching him for it, but the discovery that she had been unhappy for several weeks gave him some pain, and he hastened to assure her that he would never have tried to forward the match had he known of her distress, and that he had first had a hint of it from an intimate friend of hers, Miss King. At that, Maria stared at him in astonishment, for she could hardly believe her ears, and he was forced to repeat it two or three times. What could Mary have been thinking of? It must surely have been an error on her part, for Maria could not believe that her friend would have done such a thing out of deliberate malice. Fortunately for Miss King, Maria was not the sort to look deeply into the motives of others, for she assumed everybody was as honest and uncomplicated as herself. On this occasion she merely resolved that next time she saw Mary she would set her right in her mistake, before the rumour spread any further and caused any more harm than it had already—although it was not to be supposed that once Miss Lucas had had a little more time to think about it, she would not at last feel *some* dawning of an idea as to what had really happened, for Mary certainly had wanted him for herself, in spite of her declaration never to marry, and it was not too great a step from that knowledge to the suspicion that the rumour about Mr. Thripp must have been a deliberate attempt to further her ends.

At the close of the interview, Sir William said that he could not think of giving his consent to Maria's marrying Thomas Fairhead until he had spoken to Mr. Fairhead the elder. In the meantime, however, he promised that he should speak to Mr. Thripp, so that Maria need no longer be embarrassed by his attentions. Then he prepared—not without a heavy sigh at the prospect—to go abroad and begin the unpleasant task of spreading the news that there had been a misunderstanding with respect to the expected engagement.

The conference between Sir William and Mr. Fairhead was a long one, but not unproductive. Mr. Fairhead, still despairing at the disaster which had befallen his son (although not unsympathetic to the motives which had prompted it), was all apologies, and both men were soon in agreement: first, that it was a ridiculous and foolish engagement; second, that Thomas ought never to have had the impertinence to ask for Miss Lucas's hand at all; and third, that Maria certainly ought not to have accepted him. Furthermore, it was their respective duty as interested fathers to forbid it altogether. Having declared themselves of one accord on the matter, they then hemmed and hawed a while, and eyed one another sideways, and then Sir William ventured hesitantly that he did not like the thought of telling his daughter of their decision, for although he knew himself to be in the right, he was very fond of Maria and did not like to cause her unhappiness, for she *did* seem very much attached to Thomas Fairhead. Mr. Fairhead said in return that he was only sorry that the young people always seemed to want to have things their own way nowadays, and that it had not been like that in *his* day, but that he had observed that Thomas had been much happier since the engagement was mentioned—quite joyful, in fact—and had even been heard to make a number of quite sensible suggestions as to how he might support a wife in his present reduced state.

Having made the mutual discovery that each of them was as fond and soft-hearted as the other, Sir William and Mr. Fairhead then proceeded to debate—merely as a matter of idle supposition—how a marriage might be effected, should both of them happen to take leave of their senses long enough to give their consent to it. The first question was where the two young people should live. Mr. Fairhead would not hear of his son's joining the army, although he applauded the intention behind it. No; his place was at home with his family, for it was now more than ever necessary that they keep an eye on him, and prevent him from making any more unsuitable acquaintances. Here Mr. Fairhead mentioned a cottage in the grounds of Netherfield Park, to which Thomas had taken an unaccountable liking. It was small and quite derelict at present, but with repairs to its roof might be made tolerably comfortable at comparatively little expense, while more rooms might be added in future when money permitted. Sir William then said that Maria was a heedless girl in many respects, but that she possessed some little competence in the domestic arts, and with assistance from Lady Lucas might reasonably be trusted to learn to run a small household, such as the one Mr. Fairhead described, without mishap.

So the discussion proceeded, and by the end of it the matter had, without either of them quite knowing how, changed from idle supposition to a definite arrangement. Maria Lucas and Thomas Fairhead would be married. To be sure, neither of the two men could bring himself to call it a *very good thing*—Mr. Fairhead would have preferred his son to marry a woman of fortune, but knew that Thomas had forfeited all right to anything of the sort, while Sir William would not own his regret that Thomas was not a clergyman with a good living and a comfortable parsonage—but when Sir William told Maria that he had given his consent to the marriage, and saw his daughter's bright eyes and happy blushes, and felt her tears of joy on his hand as she wept over it, he began to think that perhaps he had not, after all, failed altogether in his duty as a father. There was much to do before the wedding could take place, however, and Sir William warned Maria that he could do very little for her, and that neither must she expect anything from the Fairheads. The first few years would be hard, but they were not the first young couple to embark upon married life with little money, and since they were neither of them burdened with extravagant tastes, there was no reason to suppose that they could not be just as happy poor as rich. Besides, Sir William had not forgotten that Mr. Fairhead had money to bequeath, and if Thomas could be induced to keep hold of it once he had it, Sir William hoped that one day he might be able to boast that his second daughter had made a better match than his first.

So Maria Lucas married Thomas Fairhead, and sooner than anybody could have guessed, for thanks to the efforts of Mr. Fairhead the elder, who had given up any hopes of assistance from Mr. Sands and had decided to act for himself, it was ascertained that not *all* of the money had been lost, and with a little struggle—and the help of a friend of Mr. Fairhead's, who had a certain influence—a larger sum than anyone had dared to hope for was recovered. So it was that Thomas and Maria found themselves with nearly two thousand pounds more than they had expected, and were able to settle into married life in their newly-repaired cottage, less than a twelvemonth after their engagement, in a certain degree of comfort, and there was not a person who saw them who did not remark on how well-suited they were, for they were both of a sort to find happiness in a simple life. Thomas never knew what a narrow escape he had had, for had he married Mary King he could never have enjoyed the peace and harmony that wedded life with Maria gave him. Meanwhile, Louisa Fairhead, having been sadly disappointed in Mary, now had to accustom herself to the idea that her brother was perfectly capable of choosing a wife for himself, and was forced to admit her fault in having originally overlooked Maria, whom she now discovered to be a very pleasant girl and much more worth knowing than she had ever before suspected. After a little struggle, she overcame her reserve and made an effort to get to know her new sister, and the two ladies quickly became very good friends—so much so that Louisa was soon able to rejoice in the happiness her brother had found, and ceased to regret the loss of Mary at all.

As for Miss King herself, she judged it better to absent herself from Hertfordshire, at least for a little while, and so she returned to her uncle's house in Liverpool, perhaps in the hope of securing one of the gentlemen she had spurned on her previous visit. Whether that were the case cannot be said; certain it is, however, that within three months after the wedding of Maria Lucas and Thomas Fairhead, the news began to circulate that Mary King had married a man some twenty years older than herself, who was reported to have an income of a thousand a year. It was less than what she had believed to be her deserts, but since all her efforts to shift for herself had failed, she judged it better to take what she could get while she still could.

The news of Maria Lucas's engagement to Thomas Fairhead came as a great surprise to the neighbourhood of Meryton, for everybody had been all but certain that she was going to marry Mr. Thripp. However, memories are mercifully short in such cases, and it was not long before it had ceased to be talked of with any great frequency; within a year or so, in fact, it had ceased to be talked of at all, and everyone was more concerned with congratulating the Fairheads on a happy arrival, and with agreeing among themselves that the family would soon outgrow their little cottage.

Mr. Thripp, meanwhile, had been mortified by the unsuccessful outcome of his courtship of Maria Lucas, but since there was still one Lucas girl to be married off, and since he still had his eye on the possible future beneficence of Lady Catherine de Bourgh, he judged it better to say nothing and pretend that it had never happened, much to the relief of Sir William Lucas, who had only uncomfortable feelings about the part he had played in the misunderstanding. Still, Mr. Thripp had at least one cause for satisfaction, for during his frequent visits to Lucas Lodge in the autumn, he had made the acquaintance of the Lucases' housekeeper, whom he had observed to be a very good, respectable sort of woman, and highly spoken of by her mistress. Thus it was that when his own dear Mrs. Partridge finally, and with great regret, informed him that she could no longer carry out her duties and would shortly retire to live with her son in

Bedfordshire, Mr. Thripp barely hesitated, and by the simple method of offering Mrs. Swale twice the wages she was accustomed to receive at Lucas Lodge, secured Mrs. Partridge's replacement within a week of her retirement. Lady Lucas was most put out at this, but since she, too, was thinking of her youngest daughter's marriage prospects, she was wise enough to overlook the offence, and to see her and Mr. Thripp talking together after church, nobody would have thought there was any bad feeling between them.

ABOUT THE AUTHOR

Clara Benson is the author of the Angela Marchmont Mysteries and Freddy Pilkington-Soames Adventures - traditional English whodunits in authentic style set in the 1920s and 30s. One day she would like to drink cocktails and solve mysteries in a sequinned dress and evening gloves. In the meantime she lives in the north of England with her family and doesn't do any of those things.

BOOKS BY CLARA BENSON

THE ANGELA MARCHMONT MYSTERIES

1. The Murder at Sissingham Hall
2. The Mystery at Underwood House
3. The Treasure at Poldarrow Point
4. The Riddle at Gipsy's Mile
5. The Incident at Fives Castle
6. The Imbroglio at the Villa Pozzi
7. The Problem at Two Tithes
8. The Trouble at Wakeley Court
9. The Scandal at 23 Mount Street
10. The Shadow at Greystone Chase
11. The Body on Archangel Beach

THE FREDDY PILKINGTON-SOAMES ADVENTURES

1. A Case of Blackmail in Belgravia
2. A Case of Murder in Mayfair
3. A Case of Conspiracy in Clerkenwell
4. A Case of Duplicity in Dorset
5. A Case of Suicide in St. James's
6. A Case of Robbery on the Riviera
7. A Case of Perplexity in Piccadilly
8. A Case of Intrigue in Islington

SHORT STORIES

Angela's Christmas Adventure

The Man on the Train

A Question of Hats

A Pinch of Strychnine

COLLECTIONS

Angela Marchmont Mysteries Books 1-3

Angela Marchmont Mysteries Books 4-6

Freddy Pilkington-Soames Adventures Books 1-3

HISTORICAL FICTION

In Darkness, Look for Stars (published by Bookouture)

The Stolen Letter (published by Bookouture)

OTHER

The Lucases of Lucas Lodge

www.ingramcontent.com/pod-product-compliance
Lightning Source LLC
Chambersburg PA
CBHW061451210726
48287CB00007B/2462